MW00436763

The Stone of Destiny:
A Sherlock Holmes Adventure

By Richard T. Ryan

Dear Gary,

Thanks for your friendship
and support. It really
is appreciated!

Rick

Hardcover ISBN 978-1-78705-082-2
Paperback ISBN 978-1-78705-083-9 epub
ISBN 978-1-78705-084-6
PDF ISBN 978-1-78705-085-3

Published in the UK by MX Publishing
335 Princess Park Manor, Royal Drive, London, N11 3GX
www.mxpublishing.co.uk

Cover design by Brian Belanger.

As always, this book is dedicated to my incredible wife, Grace, who not only does the impossible but puts up with it as well.

It is also dedicated to my daughter, Kaitlin; my son, Michael; and my son-in-law, Daniel.

Finally, this book is also dedicated to the memories of Jim Lamb and Jack Karnatski – two good men taken from us too soon.

The land's sharp features seemed to be
The Century's corpse outleant,
His crypt the cloudy canopy,
The wind his death-lament.
The ancient pulse of germ and birth
Was shrunken hard and dry,
And every spirit upon earth
Seemed fervourless as I.

The Darkling Thrush
Thomas Hardy

Introduction

Those of you who read "The Vatican Cameos" know that while on a golf holiday in Scotland with my brother not too long ago, I was unable to play the Old Course at St. Andrews when the weather refused to cooperate. As a result, I ended up attending an estate sale.

The afternoon concluded with the auctioneer placing a locked box on the block, and after a somewhat spirited bidding war, I won the auction and the box.

Upon returning to my brother's house, I took the box to his garage where I was easily able to pry off the lock. When I opened that box, I discovered a second box – a tin dispatch box – inside. After cleaning off the dirt and grime, I saw the name John H. Watson stenciled on the lid.

An examination of the contents soon proved that it was indeed the famed dispatch box that had long resided in the vaults of Cox and Company. Moreover, it was filled with manuscripts written in longhand.

The first manuscript I read was the "The Vatican Cameos," an untold tale which Dr. Watson had referenced at the beginning of "The Hound of the Baskervilles."

Having read several of the others, which will probably see the light of day in due time, I came across a folder at the very bottom of the box. It had once been secured by several rubber bands, all of which had long ago dried out and turned to dust, staining the folder, but not the manuscript.

There was no name on the folder nor on the title page, as there had been on most of the others.

Intrigued, I began to read and I can say now I know why this particular case never saw the light of the day. It was rife with political ramifications, not only for England, but for the entire British Empire at the time.

I have no idea what Dr. Watson might have titled this adventure, but I have chosen to call it, "The Stone of Destiny: A Sherlock Holmes Adventure."

Once again, my ardent hope is that you derive as much pleasure from reading this story as I did.

Richard T. Ryan

Chapter 1 – London, Jan. 23, 1901

History had turned a page.

The year 1901, the start of the new millennium, arrived with glorious celebrations around the world.

However, Holmes and I initially found our day-to-day existence little changed. Now and then Holmes would be summoned to the scene of a crime by a member of Scotland Yard. Occasionally, someone would call upon him at Baker Street. In his leisure time, he remained fond of the agony columns, his pipe and his Stradivarius.

I continued to practice medicine, covering occasionally for colleagues, and helping my friend whenever he requested my assistance.

A mere three weeks later, however, the world in which we had come of age was stilled, and the fabric ripped asunder with the passing of Queen Victoria.

She had ascended to the throne on the 20th of June 1837 and reigned as Queen of the United Kingdom of Great Britain and Ireland until her death.

In 1876, she had taken the additional title of Empress of India. During her lengthy monarchy, it was often observed that the sun never set on the British Empire.

I can assure you that on that Tuesday evening when word first began to spread of her passing, many people wondered, if indeed, the sun would have the temerity to rise the next morning.

As I walked to see a patient early the next day, it was obvious that London was a city in mourning. The news of the death of Queen Victoria had touched all of her subjects in some way, and their enormous grief could be seen writ large on the faces of Londoners of all stripes.

Hardened tradesmen and young flower girls wept openly. With no formal proclamation about the funeral, the city, it seemed, had decided to honor its Queen by adorning itself in black, to reflect the color favored by the monarch for the latter part of her lengthy reign.

When I returned home later that day, the mood in our rooms was equally somber. Over the years, Holmes and I had undertaken a number of tasks on behalf of the Crown, and we had met the Queen on more than one occasion – albeit secretly.

If for no other reason than the large V.R., which my friend had shot into the wall above the fireplace – much to Mrs. Hudson's consternation – to honor Her Majesty, I knew that Holmes had been quite fond of the Queen.

Although an air of gravity overshadowed everything, the city somehow managed to continue about its business despite the frigid January weather.

On the evening of the 24th, Holmes and I were in the sitting room smoking, neither of us saying a word, when I heard the bell ring.

Although I could discern a rather muffled conversation between Mrs. Hudson and the caller, I was unable to ascertain any of the particulars. A minute later, there was a knock on the door.

"Come in, Mrs. Hudson," said Holmes.

2

"I am so sorry to disturb you, Mr. Holmes," she said as she entered, "but you have just received this letter by messenger."

"Thank you, Mrs. Hudson," said Holmes, rising and taking an envelope from her.

"What have we here?" he said aloud as he put his pipe aside and opened the envelope. After reading it, he turned to me and said, "It is a message from my brother, Mycroft. He would like us to join him at the Diogenes Club as soon as possible. He says it is a matter of some importance."

Looking at me, he continued, "Have you plans, Watson?"

"No," I replied.

"Then may I impose upon you? After all, the message does stipulate 'you and Dr. Watson'."

As we bundled up against the chill, I wondered what Mycroft's unexpected summons might portend.

Older than Holmes, Mycroft worked in the government, and on more than one occasion, Holmes had confided in me that Mycroft, in fact, "*was* the government."

Had the weather been better, Holmes and I might have walked to the Diogenes Club, but the freezing temperatures and gusty wind forced us to hail a cab.

On the ride over we said little. I knew that Holmes abhorred speculation, so I decided I would simply have to possess my soul in patience. After paying the driver, Holmes and I entered the club and were shown into the Stranger's Room.

Easily the most unusual club in London, perhaps the world for that matter, the Diogenes Club, as Holmes had once informed me, was a club "for the most unsociable and unclubbable men" in London.

Members were not permitted to take notice of one another, and talking was absolutely forbidden, save in the Stranger's Room, where we sat waiting for Mycroft, who joined us a few minutes later.

As he settled his rather large frame into a comfortable looking wing chair that groaned slightly under his weight, he remarked, "So good of you to come. Would you care for tea, or perhaps something a bit stronger? Or shall I get right to the point?"

"Nothing for me," Holmes said, and then looking at me, inquired, "Watson?"

"Nothing for me either," I said.

"To the matter at hand then," said Mycroft. "Arrangements are being made for Queen Victoria's funeral. In fact, years ago, Victoria herself laid out in great detail exactly how the services are to be handled. She stipulated that hers is to be a military funeral, as befits the daughter of a soldier and the head of the army. She also made it quite clear that she is to be buried in a white dress, instead of the black that she has favored these many years.

"Two days hence, her sons, Edward VII and Prince Arthur, Duke of Connaught, along with her eldest grandson, the Emperor Wilhelm II of Germany, will place her body in the coffin. Her funeral will take place on Saturday, February 2, in St. George's Chapel, Windsor Castle. After two days of lying in-state, she is to be interred beside Prince Albert in Frogmore Mausoleum at Windsor Great Park."

"And what has this to do with me?" asked Holmes.

"It has come to the attention of Downing Street that certain separatist groups in both Ireland and Scotland may attempt to turn this sad occasion to their advantage. As you know, there has been an increased cry for independence from both lands, though louder by far from Ireland. What better time to press your case than at the state funeral of a monarch?

"We have good reason to believe that the threats are real; unfortunately, what is not so clear, is the shape they may take," continued Mycroft.

"And am I now to be a bodyguard to the King?" asked Holmes with just the slightest hint of impatience.

"Of course not," said Mycroft amiably. "We would simply like you to be present at Queen Victoria's funeral and in the days and hours before. If you should see something or someone suspicious, you and Dr. Watson can either handle it as you see fit, or you may turn it over to Scotland Yard. We would also like you to precede the funeral to Frogmore and examine that as you would any crime scene before the cortege arrives."

"As you wish," said Holmes. "In a very real sense, Victoria will always be my Queen, and to see that she is laid to rest without disruption is the least I can do."

"Splendid," said Mycroft. "I shall tell the Home Office as well as Scotland Yard that you are to be given *carte blanche*."

"Thank you," said Holmes.

Mycroft then handed Holmes a letter that he had quite obviously penned in advance. "Just present this and you will have immediate entrée to any area of the palace or the castle that you might wish to inspect."

"Am I that predictable?" asked Holmes.

"Not at all," replied Mycroft. "But I am well aware of how fond you were of Her Highness, and I know you wouldn't want anything to mar the arrangements."

As we rode back to Baker Street in the cab, I was thinking that this was certainly an assignment far beneath my friend's talents. Rest assured, I had no idea at the time how badly I was mistaken.

Chapter 2 – London, Jan. 24 – Feb. 2

The next morning I awoke and dressed, and when I entered the sitting room, I found Holmes reading a newspaper.

"It appears that crime itself has come to a halt out of respect for the Queen. There is nothing in any of the papers that would warrant our attention, so I suppose Mycroft's request will serve as a diversion of sorts, if nothing else. Now, let us enjoy some breakfast and then make our way to Buckingham Palace."

As we ate, Holmes informed me, "The Queen's body will arrive from the Isle of Wight on the royal yacht, Alberta, this morning, and it will then be transported to London via train. After the last-minute details have been attended to at the palace, she is to be taken to Windsor on Saturday on a carriage pulled by eight white horses."

After finishing, we took a carriage to the palace, where Mycroft proved as good as his word. After presenting the letter, Holmes and I practically had the run of the place. Holmes carefully examined the room where the final preparations before the journey to Windsor were to occur. After considering sight-lines from the windows and ascertaining the heightened security that would be on hand, Holmes pronounced everything safe and secure.

As we left the palace and hailed a cab for the long ride to Windsor, Holmes confided to me, "I do think this is a fool's errand. There will be untold thousands of people lining the entire parade route, and the cortege will include brigades of military men, both infantry and cavalry. I should think that would be protection enough."

He paused before continuing, "Still, I have promised Mycroft, and so we will carry out our due diligence."

St George's Chapel, where the funeral was to take place, is approximately 21 miles from Buckingham Palace in London. Holmes told the driver the route he wanted him to follow, and before long, we were heading out of the city on High Street.

The arrangements called for Queen Victoria to lie in state for two days, and then she was to be interred next to her beloved Albert at the Frogmore Mausoleum at Windsor Great Park. I found it odd that the Queen had eschewed burial at Westminster Abbey, but thought little of it at the time.

After nearly three hours, we arrived at Windsor Castle. Again, all doors were opened to us as soon as Holmes presented Mycroft's letter. We examined the chapel first, then we walked the grounds and finally we visited the mausoleum.

"If an attack or an event of some sort is planned," said Holmes, "it will not occur here. I believe that I can report that to Mycroft with absolute certainty and save us a return trip here, unless, of course, you should desire to attend the funeral, Watson."

"I think I should feel very out of place," I said truthfully.

"As would I," said Holmes. "Let us grieve and honor the Queen in our own heartfelt way."

After we had returned to London, Holmes drafted a detailed report, with one or two suggestions, and sent it by messenger to Mycroft.

Over the next several days, the pace of the city remained sluggish and then on Saturday, the day of the funeral, it was as though London's heart had ceased beating altogether.

Few shops were open during the day, and I can only assume that both business owners and their employees had descended on the route to Windsor in an effort to pay their final respects to their beloved monarch.

Holmes was gone for most of the day, and he didn't return until late in the afternoon. When I asked him where he had been, he said that he had spent the morning honoring his Queen. When he didn't elaborate, I thought it prudent not to press the issue.

After dinner, I heard the strains of the violin coming from his room, so I decided to read for a while and then turn in early.

At dawn the next day, I was called away to tend to a patient. I returned mid-morning, and I must have dozed off in my chair. Suddenly, I was awakened by Holmes shaking my shoulder and telling me, "Come, Watson. We have been summoned by Mycroft, and unless I miss my guess, it is a matter of utmost urgency."

I grabbed my coat, and then Holmes and I hailed a cab and told the driver to take us to the Diogenes Club.

Chapter 3 – London, Feb. 2

Big Ben had just struck four.

Denis Lyons stood in the small undercroft. Surrounding him were three other members of the Irish Republican Brotherhood – James Santry, Edward Nesbitt and John O'Brien.

"So, they want to celebrate the hundredth anniversary of their beloved Act of Union," Lyons sneered. "We'll give them something to think about this night, my boys."

"British bastards," said O'Brien. "They are free, but we shall never be? Surely, God would not allow such an abomination to continue."

"All we need is the all-clear sign from Michael, and we can get to work," Lyons said.

O'Brien pulled out a small flask and said, "I'll drink to that."

"Put that away," exclaimed Lyons, "There'll be time enough to celebrate after we've concluded our business."

A chagrined O'Brien returned the flask to his pocket – unopened.

A few minutes later, young Michael Collins entered the room.

"What say ye boy?" asked Lyons.

"The church is locked tight, but I did see two Bobbies. One is standing on Abingdon Street, not too far from the entrance to Cromwell's Green. The other is further up Abingdon, standing almost in front of the Jewel Tower."

"How about the sides and the rear?" asked Lyons. "Did you look there as well?"

"Yes sir," replied Michael, "and I saw no one but the two coppers."

"You have done well, my boy. Here's a little something for your trouble," he said, giving the boy a shilling.

"That's not necessary," said Santry.

"Good work should be rewarded," replied Lyons," and he has done a splendid job. Now, Michael, you go back to the boarding house and wait for us. I don't want you involved in this part of the operation."

"But I can help," exclaimed the boy.

"You already have," said Lyons, "and you may yet again, but now is not your time. I know they call you 'The Big Fella' at home, but tonight, we need the strong fellows."

"I'm strong," protested the youngster.

"I'm sure you are laddy," said Lyons, "but I don't want you involved – just in case this goes south. Your mother would never forgive me. Do you understand?"

The boy nodded.

Turning to the rest of his crew, Lyons said, "I wish you all had his spirit. Are you ready?"

They grunted assent.

"Do you have the pipes?" asked Lyons.

"They're in the wagon," replied Santry.

"And the other thing?"

"That's hidden in the wagon as well," said O'Brien.

"Well, we must be very careful with it," said Lyons. "Without that, this is nothing but an exercise in futility."

The four men left the undercroft, and Lyons and Santry climbed into the front of the wagon while O'Brien and Nesbitt rode in the rear. With Santry holding the reins, they drove slowly along Great College Street and then turned left toward Westminster Abbey. They were all wearing dark suits, and they looked as though they might have been part of a small funeral cortege.

Slowly, they drove onto the grounds and approached a little used side door, far back from the main entrance.

A blacksmith, Santry had dealt with a great many locks in his career, and he'd fashioned many different skeleton keys on the off-chance they might be needed.

From his pocket he took a large ring. All the keys on it had been wrapped in cloth so as to muffle any jingling sound they might make.

On the third try, the key turned smoothly and opened the lock.

The four of them then carried the coffin, in which they had placed the pipes and the other necessary items, from the wagon.

Once they were inside the church, they lit two dark lanterns and headed straight for the Chapel of St. Edward the Confessor.

When they had reached it, they opened the coffin and O'Brien took out the tools that he needed. Within minutes, the four had done what they needed to do, and they left with Lyons and Santry leading the way and O'Brien and Nesbitt following behind.

When they had loaded the wagon, Santry carefully closed and locked the door to the abbey. After a 10-minute drive, during which they all sat in silence, they found themselves back in their rooms where young Michael was waiting for them.

No sooner had they entered, then he said, "You did it! You did it! Can I see it please?"

"Of course, my lad," said Lyons, "It's in the wagon. One peek and then to bed. We have to leave for home in a few hours, and I want to put as much distance between us and this accursed country as possible. There's a train leaving for Liverpool at one, and I intend to be on it."

"So one quick look then" he continued, "and then you must get some sleep."

He took the boy outside and carefully pried the nails from the lid. As he lifted it, he watched as Michael's grin grew bigger and bigger.

"This will teach them," the youngster exclaimed.

"And now to sleep," said Lyons. "This is only the beginning of our journey. I'll wait here, Michael. Tell Mr. Nesbitt that he has the first watch."

"Yes sir," said the youngster, saluting as he scurried inside.

Chapter 4 – London, February 2

For the second time in a week, Holmes and I had been summoned by Mycroft to the Diogenes Club.

We arrived just after 10:30 a.m. and had barely taken our seats in the Stranger's Room, when Mycroft entered. His usual unflappable demeanor was absent, and I thought I detected just a hint of urgency in his voice.

"Thank you for coming," he said. "I hate to summon you on such a day as this, but you are my only hope."

Holmes said, "Come now, it can't be as bad as all that."

"Oh, but it is," said Mycroft. "They have taken the stone."

"To whom are you referring," said Holmes, "And what stone is it that *they* have taken?"

"I must confess that I do not know who they are," said Mycroft, "although I am inclined to think they are either Scottish separatists or Irish nationalists. I am more disposed to believe it is the latter since this is the centenary of the Acts of Union."

"Are you going to tell me that the Coronation Stone has been taken from Westminster?" asked Holmes incredulously.

"I am afraid so," said Mycroft miserably. "Sometime early this morning while everyone was at Windsor preparing for Queen Victoria's funeral, thieves took advantage of the lull in security to break into Westminster Abbey to steal the Stone of Destiny."

"It can't have been easy," I said, "it must weigh at least 200 pounds."

"Actually, doctor," said Mycroft, "It weighs exactly 336 pounds."

"If memory serves, it's not all that big," said Holmes.

"Having come to understand that all knowledge is grist for your mill, I have anticipated your question. The Stone of Scone – or the Stone of Destiny or the Coronation Stone, as it is more widely known – measures exactly 26 inches by 16 and three-quarter inches by 10 and a half inches. A rough cross has been carved into one surface, and iron rings have been embedded near either end to aid with transport."

"So it could easily be concealed in a trunk or a large piece of luggage," observed Holmes.

"I suppose so," said Mycroft, "as long it were being carried by an extremely strong man."

"How did you discover that it was missing?" asked Holmes.

17

"One of the caretakers took it upon himself to clean the Coronation Chair and see what repairs it might require for King Edward's coronation. As he braced himself to push the chair away from the wall, he noticed that it moved quite easily. When he examined the stone, he discovered that it had been replaced by a very clever papier-mâché counterfeit. But for his diligence, the theft might have gone unnoticed for weeks, perhaps months."

"Oh, I'm quite certain you would have heard from the thieves before too long," observed Holmes drily.

"I'm sure you are right," agreed Mycroft.

"If I go to Westminster now, am I liable to find anything, or has Scotland Yard been trampling all over the scene, obliterating any clues that might have been left behind?"

"Once the theft was discovered, both the chapel and the abbey were sealed," said Mycroft. "No one knows of this catastrophe, but more important, no one must learn of it. It would cause a national scandal."

"So who does know?" asked my friend.

"Only the caretaker and the Dean of Westminster, George Bradley, who had enough sense to close the church immediately and then inform me," said Mycroft. "I have known Bradley a great many years, and he is the soul of discretion. In fact, he is detaining the caretaker until he hears from me."

"Bravo," said Holmes. "Watson and I shall go to Westminster immediately, and see what clues, if any, we may uncover."

"In the meantime," Holmes continued, "You must let it be known as soon as possible, albeit discreetly, that all trunks and other large pieces of luggage are to be thoroughly inspected before they can be put on a train or a ship."

"It will be done immediately," said Mycroft.

"I don't suppose it is possible to close the borders," mused Holmes.

"I could do that as well," replied Mycroft, "but we run the risk of an international incident. We would also tip our hand to the thieves that we have tumbled to their deception so quickly. Should that happen, who knows what action they might take."

"True," said Holmes. "For now, let us sit and wait and watch, and when they make the next move, we will be ready to respond.

"Now, Watson, we are off to Westminster," exclaimed my friend.

Chapter 5 – London, Feb. 2

"We have to visit just one place on our way to the station," said Lyons. "I know it's rather early, but we are expected."

Before they left their rooms, Lyons went ahead to see what other guests were awake. When he returned and said no one was stirring, Nesbitt and Santry each made their way to where O'Brien was now standing guard by the wagon.

Lyons and Michael carried the other bags out, and a few minutes later, they were on Edgware Road, where they made a single stop and picked up a brushed brass plaque that O'Brien neatly affixed to the lid of the coffin with four wood screws.

"That's a bit of brilliance, Denis," said O'Brien as Nesbitt nodded in assent.

"Even if they are looking, which I doubt they are, I do not think they will look in there," Lyons remarked.

After just a short drive, they arrived at the Liverpool Street Station. As the men climbed down, they separated, each to buy his own ticket.

Lyons, Santry and young Michael remained with the stone, which they lifted onto a porter's dolly.

At the ticket window, Lyons said, "I need two tickets for the next train to Liverpool. We are bringing my sister home to bury her in Ireland."

After expressing his condolences, the clerk told Lyons the cost was 17 shillings each for third class and 10 shillings for his "sister" to ride in the cargo car. When asked, the clerk said the journey would take approximately eight hours.

After heading over to the right track and slipping the conductor a few shillings, Lyons obtained permission to ride in the cargo car so that he could grieve for his beloved sister.

As two porters lifted the coffin into the car, one remarked to the other, "Jesus, she weighs a ton. I guess she must have liked her own cooking."

The other tried to suppress a laugh, and Lyons pretended that he hadn't heard the comment.

After they had placed the coffin in the car, Lyons slipped them a few more shillings. A short while later, he saw a police officer approach the porters.

"Are you checking all the large trunks as I instructed you?" he asked.

At that point, Lyons, who was sitting in the car and could not be seen by the officer, listened intently, fearing for a second that all might be lost.

"We are, sir," said one of the porters. "And so far, we have nothing to report."

"Keep up the good work, men," he advised.

Shortly before one, Santry and Michael took seats in the closest car, and a few minutes later O'Brien boarded the train and sat at the other end of the car. Just as the train was about to leave, Nesbitt pulled himself aboard, and the journey to Liverpool had begun.

The trip was long and tedious, and after an hour had passed, Michael asked Santry if he might join Mr. Lyons in the cargo car.

"I have no objections if he has none," said Santry.

As Michael entered the cargo car, he saw Lyons sitting on the floor next to the coffin, reading a book.

"I'm glad you are here, Michael. I could use the company," Lyons said, putting the youngster at ease.

After checking to make certain they were alone, Michael asked, "Will you tell me about the stone again, Mr. Lyons? And why does it have so many names?"

"To answer your first question, I'd be happy to. As for your second question, perhaps that will become clear as I answer your first."

"By what names, do you know it, Michael?"

"I have heard it called the Stone of Destiny, the Stone of Scone and the Coronation Stone," the youngster replied.

"It has several other names as well," said Lyons. "I have also heard it referred to as Jacob's Pillow, the *Lia Fáil* and the Tanist Stone.

"While the origins of the stone are shrouded in mystery, the legend that I choose to believe says that in biblical times, the Stone of Destiny was used as a pillow by Jacob as he fled from his brother, Esau.

"Supposedly, it traveled with the Israelites in the wilderness for 40 years and was the source of their water. It was brought to Ireland hundreds of years before Christ was born by the prophet, Jeremiah. Once it was here, it was set up on the hills of Tara, where it was called the *Lia Fáil* and all the ancient kings of Ireland were crowned there.

"When the Celtic Scots invaded and occupied Ireland, under the leadership of Cináed mac Ailpín, whom you know as Kenneth MacAlpin, he had the stone brought to Scone, where he was crowned king in 840. It was then used as part of the crowning ceremonies for the kings of Dalriada, in the west of Scotland.

"John Balliol was the last Scottish king to be crowned on the stone at Scone in 1292."

Lyons paused to see what effect his words were having on the boy.

24

"So the stone is rightfully ours then?" asked the youngster.

"Indeed it is lad. Would you like to hear how the tale ends?"

"I would," said the boy.

"At the end of the 13th century, the British King, Edward I, decided to seize control of Scotland. So the monarch, who was known as 'Longshanks' because of his height and 'The Hammer of the Scots' because of his prowess in battle, invaded in 1296 and seized the stone and other Scottish relics and had them taken to Westminster Abbey. Several years later, he had a special throne called the 'Coronation Chair' constructed, and the stone was placed inside it."

"The stone was in the chair?" the boy asked,

Nodding, Lyons continued, "Yes. King Edward saw it as a symbolic way of telling the world that the kings of England were also the kings of Scotland. Since that time, every British monarch has sat in the Coronation Chair and thus upon the Stone of Scone, or as they like to call it the Coronation Stone, when they are invested."

Lyons paused for effect, "But I tell you this, Michael. If the next King of England hopes to carry on that tradition, he must be willing to make some serious concessions."

Chapter 6 – London, Feb. 2

Holmes and I took a cab to Westminster where we met George Bradley in the Church House, which had been finished just five years earlier.

Upon opening the front door, Bradley looked at my friend and inquired, "You are Mr. Sherlock Holmes?"

When my friend nodded, Bradley exclaimed, "Mr. Holmes, I cannot tell you how relieved I am to see you."

Holmes then introduced me, and Bradley said, "Were this day not marred by tragedy, I should be very happy to make the acquaintance of both of you. However, our Queen is gone, and now the Coronation Stone has been stolen."

"Who else knows about the theft?" asked Holmes.

"Only Mr. Dodge, the caretaker who discovered the theft. I have kept him here, and I have had the church and grounds secured. I am familiar with your methods, Mr. Holmes. I can only hope that I have acted quickly enough."

"You have done splendidly," my friend assured him. "Now, I should very much like to speak with your Mr. Dodge."

Bradley led us into a small sitting room where we found a man of about 50 sitting by the fireplace. He rose when we entered and said, "You must be Sherlock Holmes."

"Guilty as charged," replied Holmes. "Now, would you mind if I asked you a few questions?"

"If I answer them, can I go home for lunch?" he replied. "I'm sure my missus is worried sick."

"Then I shall be as quick as I can," said Holmes. "How long have you worked at the abbey?"

"I started here 19 years ago," he replied.

"And what exactly are your duties?"

"I do general maintenance – painting, cleaning and such," he replied. "And in the warmer weather, I tend to the plants and gardens."

"And how did you come to discover the Coronation Stone was missing?" asked Holmes.

"I thought that with the Queen passing, we would soon be having a coronation here. She last used the Coronation Chair in 1887, during her golden jubilee year." He paused and then asked, "Have you ever seen the Coronation Chair, Mr. Holmes?"

"Only from a distance," my friend replied.

"Well, over the years, the students from the school and some visitors as well, I suppose, have carved their initials and names into the back of it. There are also scratches on the arms. I thought I would try to repair it as best I could. So I brought my cleaning supplies with me, and when I went to push the chair farther out from the wall so that I could see the back better, it slid right out. That's when I knew something was amiss.

"When I looked closely at the Coronation Stone, I soon realized it wasn't the stone at all, but some sort of imitation. So I went straightaway and found Mr. Bradley, and we then ushered everyone out of the church, saying that repairs to the roof had to be made immediately. We locked all the doors; Mr. Bradley informed the authorities, and I've been here ever since."

"And you didn't notice anything unusual? You saw nothing suspicious?"

"No sir," said Dodge.

"Well then, I am sorry you had to go through this," said Holmes, "But you have done well."

Holmes then tried to hand the man a five-shilling coin.

"I can't accept that," said Dodge.

"Please, buy your wife some flowers," Holmes said. "But whatever you do, you must not repeat any of this to anyone. Right now, secrecy is our greatest ally."

"You have my word, Mr. Holmes," he said. "Mr. Bradley, shall I come back after lunch?"

"No, Mr. Dodge, take the rest of the day off, and I will see you in the morning."

Bradley walked him to the front door and then rejoined us. "He's a good man," the dean said.

"Yes, I think you are quite lucky to have him," said Holmes.

"Now, I should very much like to see the church and the grounds," said Holmes. "Since it is rather overcast, have you any torches, Mr. Bradley? And a blanket?"

"I shall get them," he said. A minute later he returned with three of the new electric hand torches that were just coming on the market and a thick woolen blanket. "I hope these will suffice," he said.

"I am sure they will," said Holmes, who then led us out the door and headed for the side of Westminster Abbey.

"I rather doubt they came through the main entrance," said Holmes. "Let us go to the north doorway first."

As we approached the massive door, Holmes cautioned us to stay a few feet to the side of the path and to be careful not to step on the ground directly next to it if possible.

"I want to check both the ground and this path to see if they have been kind enough to leave any footprints," he informed us.

Holmes then spread the blanket out on the ground and threw himself upon it. With his lens, he began to examine a section of the path.

"They arrived in a wagon drawn by two horses, one of which needs a new shoe on its left rear hoof," he said. "When they departed, they were carrying something quite heavy in the wagon as you can see by the deeper ruts in the mud."

Even without a close examination, I could make out the wheel ruts coming from the church, though how Holmes spotted those going to it escaped me. When we arrived at the door, Holmes instructed Bradley and me to shine our lights on the lock as we were now standing in a deep shadow. "There are no signs of forced entry that I can discern, which makes me think they had a key."

"That's impossible, Mr. Holmes," spluttered Bradley.

At the word "impossible," Holmes looked at me knowingly and then fixed his gaze on Bradley. "Well then Mr. Bradley, how did they get in? Nothing has been broken; the lock is intact and appears to be working. Do you have a key, sir?" he asked.

Bradley produced a large ring from his pocket and after examining several keys, let the others fall and said, "This is the key for that door."

"Mr. Bradley, looking at this key and that lock, I can say only that older isn't always better. If I wished, I could pick this lock in just a moment or two. Although the horse is out of the barn, I strongly suggest that you consider replacing your present locks with something a bit more secure. In addition, you might also consider hiring a night watchman and installing him in the abbey."

With that, Holmes opened the door with Bradley's key, and we stepped inside the abbey.

Even in semi-darkness, the majesty of Westminster Abbey was obvious. We made our way past the chapels of St. Andrew, St. Michael and St. John the Evangelist. Directly across from the Islips Chapel is the Chapel of Edward the

Confessor, and Holmes immediately headed for the Coronation Chair.

As Bradley and I looked on, he examined the chair with his lens, and then, without much effort, slid it about a foot.

He then knelt and examined the wood framework that had surrounded the stone.

"I think one of the men involved must be a carpenter," he said,

"You can see by the fresh marks here and there," he said pointing to the sides of the bottom of the chair, "that this piece has been very carefully removed and then reinserted. It seems rather obvious that it had to be taken out in order to gain access to the stone."

Holmes asked me to pull on one of the front legs of the chair and Bradley on the other. With our help he was able to dislodge the piece of the wood and carefully remove the papier-mâché Stone of Destiny from its resting place.

"From what little I remember of the stone, this appears to be quite a good likeness," Holmes remarked.

"It is quite like it," Bradley said.

"Mr. Bradley, the first thing in the morning – even before you open the abbey – you are to remove the Coronation Chair and hide it. Should anyone ask, you can tell them it is being cleaned and restored for King Edward's pending coronation."

Bradley nodded, "I'll get Mr. Dodge to help me. We shall put it in the triforium. I think it will just fit in the narrow staircase."

"Triforium?" I asked.

"That's a splendid suggestion," said Holmes.

Pointing up to the darkened ceiling, Holmes said to me, "You can just about see it now, but there is a small gallery up there, right below the clerestory windows. It is closed to the public, and, if I recall, the only way in is through the private door in the Poets' Corner."

"Mr. Holmes, I am surprised at how much you know about the church."

"I expect that I shall know even more before long," he replied drily.

"Now, I have one more request, Mr. Bradley."

"Anything," he replied.

"Can you fetch us a large sack, Watson and I will be taking this stone with us."

After Bradley had left, I said to Holmes, "I know there must be a clue in there, but for the life of me…"

Holmes cut me off saying, "A clue? Watson, when they left this behind, they might as well have handed me their calling card."

Chapter 7 – Liverpool, Feb. 2

"Wake up, Michael. We're here," said Lyons, shaking the boy.

They had finally arrived in Liverpool, and although it was evening, the station was teeming with people. Michael watched as Lyons, Santry and Nesbitt lifted the coffin down from the cargo car. A few minutes later, O'Brien joined them.

"I've a wagon that will take us to the docks," he said.

"We must be very careful," Lyons whispered. "They know the stone has been taken, and they are inspecting all trunks. We must hope our luck holds."

So they carefully hoisted the coffin on their shoulders and carried it through the station like pallbearers.

They gently placed the coffin in the rear of the wagon, and then Lyons sat up front with the driver while the others took their places in the back.'

After telling the driver to take them to the Isle of Man Steam Packet Company docks, everyone lapsed into silence and young Michael began to weep softly.

The driver looked at Michael and then at Santry.

"There, there, lad," Santry comforted him. "She is in a better place."

When they arrived at the docks, Lyons booked passage for them all on the Tynwald, the same ship on which they had crossed a few days earlier.

Michael could hardly hide his disappointment. He had been hoping to return home on the much newer and faster Prince of Wales. Lyons told him that ship wasn't sailing for two more days and the passage was quite dear compared to the Tynwald.

As the porter approached, Michael resumed his weeping.

"What's all this?" the porter asked solicitously.

"My sister, his mother, has passed, and we are bringing her home to Ireland," said Lyons.

"My deepest condolences," said the porter.

After slipping the man a few pounds, Lyons was assured that he would be able to ride in the hold with his sister if he so desired, and the boy would be able to sit with his mother as well.

"I hope you have your sea legs, sir," the porter said. "If the waves are is rough, this ship pitches something terrible."

"We'll be fine, Lyons assured him. "And you say we shall reach Cobh in approximately eighteen hours?"

"If the ship doesn't dally in Dublin, and the water is calm, perhaps even a bit less," said the porter.

After they had boarded, Lyons told the men to go to the cabin and then to eat. "And when you've finished, could one of you bring us something?"

"I will," said O'Brien.

After they had left, Lyons said to Michael, "The tears were a bit of genius my boy."

"I'm just trying to help," said the youngster.

"And so you have, Michael. Ireland would be proud of you."

Finally, after another hour had passed, the anchor was lifted, and the Tynwald set sail for Ireland.

Chapter 8 – London, Feb. 2-3

After we had returned to Baker Street with the faux stone, Holmes immediately set about analyzing it. Knowing that I would be of little use to my friend once he became engrossed in his scientific endeavors, I decided to take in a show and settled on "A Chinese Honeymoon."

There was a touring company in London, and I must admit that I enjoyed the comedy immensely.

As I ascended the stairs to our rooms, I could smell the results of Holmes' labors, and I paused for a second and considered enjoying a nightcap at a nearby pub. However, my curiosity got the better of me, so despite the malodorous condition of our lodgings, I pushed open the door. Holmes was peering at something intently through his microscope. So engrossed was he that for a second I thought he might not have heard me enter.

Without looking up, he asked me, "So, how was the show?"

"How could you possibly know where I have been?" I asked.

He turned to me and smiled, "It is now 10:22. With intermission, the average show runs approximately two hours. Allowing an extra five minutes for a crowded theater, and then deducting two minutes from the normal walking time of 13 minutes to stroll to the West End on a balmy summer night, that should put you here right about now."

I chuckled, "You never cease to amaze me, Holmes."

"And is 'A Chinese Honeymoon' as amusing as they say?"

"Now, you go too far," I said.

"What on earth do you mean?"

"Either you followed me or had someone do it. There is no way that you could know which play I went to see otherwise."

"I could if I looked at the playbill protruding from your pocket," he laughed.

I looked down and there it was, sticking out of my coat pocket. "I apologize, Holmes," I said.

"No need for that, old man."

"Well, let me see if I can repay you in kind. I can see that you have made some progress, but there are still several things that elude you; otherwise, you would not still be at your experiments."

"Bravo, Watson!" he exclaimed.

"I do believe that I have made some small headway, but the extent has yet to be determined."

"Why do you say that?" I asked.

"Thus far the stone has yielded precious little. I am afraid that I was more than a bit premature when I likened it to a calling card."

He continued, "The chicken wire that was used for the frame was manufactured by Barnard, Bishop & Barnard."

"Well that is surely a clue that we can follow," I said.

"I'm afraid not," Holmes replied. "It is the most common type available and can be purchased at any number of ironmongers throughout the city.

"I thought the materials in the papier-mâché might offer an avenue worth exploring, but again, they are all of the most common types and can be obtained at any decent emporium. Even the paint used is widely available."

"So what then have you discovered?" I asked.

"Consider the stone itself for a second, Watson. The thieves were hoping their substitution would pass muster for who knows how long. So this wasn't just cobbled together. The more I examined it, the more I became convinced that this was created by an artist. The edges have all been neatly trimmed. There is no wasted material, and everything has been formed and molded just so.

"So, then I had to ask myself, how many people in London are capable of producing such a piece, and after a bit of thought and some research, I was able to compile a list of three names.

"There is a young man, Ernst Granger, with a shop on High Street, who was an apprentice under Ludwig Grenier. A second young man, Daniel McCormick, is employed by Asprey and Co. in New Bond Street. The third person is a woman, Kathleen McMahon, who works at Madame Tussaud's on Marylebone Road."

"If Mycroft is correct about Irish nationalists, then the last two names – McCormick and McMahon – are quite telling, are they not?" I suggested.

"They may be, but let's not jump to conclusions until we have met and interviewed them.

"Now, let us enjoy that nightcap you were considering and then to bed," said Holmes.

"I'm not even going to ask," I laughed.

"He who hesitates on the stairs is usually weighing other options," said Holmes. "Considering the hour, I believe yours were rather limited," he added.

The next morning, we awoke and after breakfast made our way to High Street where we discovered that Ernst Granger had closed his shop about a year ago and then returned to Germany.

Next, we headed over to New Bond Street. In business for more than a century, Asprey & Co is generally regarded as one of London's foremost shops, offering "articles of exclusive design and high quality, whether for personal adornment or personal accompaniment and to endow with richness and beauty the table and homes of people of refinement and discernment."

I was quite familiar with the store, having purchased several items for my first wife there.

As we entered, George, the manager, greeted us, "Dr. Watson, it has been a long time since you have graced us with your presence. How may I be of service?"

"George, this is my friend, Mr. Sherlock Holmes."

"The one about whom you so often write?" asked George incredulously. "And all these years, I thought he was just a fiction. Mr. Holmes, I am delighted to meet you."

"I am quite real, I assure you, sir," said my friend coolly. Leaning in, Holmes said to him in a subdued tone of voice, "Were I not, how else would I know that you have had a terrible row with your wife this morning? And that if you keep up your dalliance with that sales clerk, she is going to leave you."

"Mr. Holmes," he whispered, his façade of bonhomie, shattered. "How could you possibly know?"

"Sir, you manage one of the most esteemed stores in London. Yet your shoes are not shined, your tie is askew and your eyes are puffy and red as though you have been weeping. No self-respecting woman would let a man of your position leave the house looking as you do, unless she were quite angry with him."

Plucking two strands of long, blonde hair, one from each of George's shoulders, Holmes continued, "And unless I am greatly mistaken, these belong to that rather attractive young woman over there, who I can only assume has been comforting you."

"What am I to do, Mr. Holmes?" asked George.

"For matters of the heart, I suggest you consult Dr. Watson. As for me, I should like very much to speak with your Mr. McCormick if he is available."

"I'll fetch him immediately," said George, who returned a moment later with a young man of about thirty in tow.

After George had introduced us, he said, "If you should like to speak in private, please use my office, Mr. Holmes."

"Thank you," said Holmes, "and while I am chatting with Mr. McCormick here, Watson, why don't you and George enjoy some tea and engage in a bit of soul-searching at that little shop just outside the other entrance, on Albemarle Street. I will join you as soon as I am finished."

Although I would have preferred to stay with Holmes, I soldiered on and listened to George's tale of infatuation and woe.

When he had finished, I said, "I have but one question: Do you still love your wife?"

When he nodded, I said, "Then you know what you must do. You must make a clean break of it. Give the young lady a glowing letter of recommendation, a generous severance and make certain that she has a new position. If you do that, you will find yourself a happier man."

At that moment, Holmes joined us. "I trust Dr. Watson has been able to assist you," said my friend, "and I should like to say that young McCormick has a bright future, but I don't think you are making full use of his abilities."

"Thank you, Mr. Holmes," exclaimed George. "And thank you, Dr. Watson."

"I'm glad to see that you were able to help George," Holmes said, smiling at me. "Somehow, I knew you would be up to the task."

"How did your interview with Mister McCormick go?" I asked.

"Quite well. He is a very sharp young man, who may one day replace George, if your friend fails to get his affairs in order.

"And now, let us pay a call at Madame Tussaud's, where I am sure we will be warmly received by John Theodore, and I can only hope that we shall find Kathleen McMahon in her workshop."

Chapter 9 – Southern Ireland, Feb. 3-4

During most of the voyage, young Michael sat spellbound as Lyons told him again of the Irish kings and the various legends surrounding both the *Lia Fail* or Irish Stone of Destiny and the Stone of Scone or Scottish Stone of Destiny.

Finally, Lyons told Michael to go the cabin and get some sleep. The youngster reluctantly agreed.

When the Tynwald finally arrived in Cobh, near Cork, Michael had to be awakened, but none of the men teased him about falling asleep, for despite his age, they all respected him, and they all believed that Michael Collins had a bright future in front of him in the Irish Republican Brotherhood.

After the boat had docked, the men carried the coffin to a wagon. As they set out along Spy Hill past the Old Church, Lyons told Michael that when he arrived home he was to swear his family to secrecy and then tell them how his tears had helped save the day and aided in the struggle to make Ireland free.

When they arrived in Clonakilty, several hours later, they stopped by Michael's house. As the youngster stepped down, Lyons said, "I shall see you tomorrow. Right now, I have some serious work to do, and for your own good, lad, I'm keeping you in the dark."

Michael knew his protests would fall on deaf ears, so he went into the house where he found his mother and all his brothers and sisters waiting for him.

As he told them of his adventure in London and the theft of the Coronation Stone, they sat rapt. Finally, when he had finished, his sister, Helena, said, "Michael, we are all so very proud of you, but you are going to confess to Father Malachi that you helped steal the stone, are you not?"

At that they all laughed, and Michael promised his sister, who was bent on becoming a nun, that come Saturday he would be properly shriven.

* * *

After dropping the boy off, Lyons and his men headed north to Beal na Blath where they started west to Macroon. When they arrived at Balleyvourney, it was the middle of the night and almost no one was stirring, but a member of the Brotherhood was waiting for them with fresh horses.

After they had crossed into County Kerry, Santry broke the prolonged silence by asking, "How on Earth did you ever think of this place?"

"I was raised near Muckross and educated by Franciscans. They would always talk of the abbey and its importance in the history of Killarney and Ireland. Best of all for our purposes, it is distant enough from Clonakilty yet still accessible. Moreover, I do not think any agents of the Crown are apt to be looking where we're going to be hiding it," said Lyons.

"And where would that be?" asked O'Brien.

"All in due time," replied Lyons.

Eventually they passed Loo Bridge and the sight of the train tracks prompted Nesbitt to inquire, "Why didn't we take the train here? Surely, it would've been much easier and faster."

"True enough," said Lyons, "but I am known here. If anyone were to see me with a coffin, I would certainly have some explaining to do. And if the police should ever tumble to how we got the stone out of England, don't you think they'd be questioning every porter in Eire? And while there are some that we can trust, there are just as many, if not more, would turn us in for some British sovereigns."

After another 30 minutes, they arrived at the churchyard of Muckross Abbey.

"Don't you think it is fitting?" asked Lyons, "We take the stone from their abbey and place it in ours. I find a certain poetic justice in that."

They had stopped in a large courtyard. It was a clear night and in the moonlight, the ruins of the abbey were easy to make out as was a large yew tree that towered over the surrounding landscape.

"Now what?" asked O'Brien. "Do we just leave it here?"

"Of course not," said Lyons, "Where do coffins usually go?"

"In the ground?" ventured Nesbitt.

"In the ground," repeated Lyons. "Just over there is Muckross Cemetery. It is still active today, and if you believe

46

in legends, it is the burial site of many of the O'Donoghue chieftains."

He added, "In this instance, I don't think they will mind an interloper."

They drove across the courtyard to a remote corner of the cemetery, and then they all took shovels and lanterns from the wagon.

"Try to be careful with the sod," Lyons told them. "We must replace it so that this looks as undisturbed as is possible. After all, it wouldn't do to have a freshly dug grave in an old section of a cemetery like this. Especially when you see what I have planned for it."

"And what is that?" asked Nesbitt.

"And spoil the surprise?" asked Lyons. "You'll find out soon enough."

And so they set to their task. The earth was cold and hard and the digging difficult. When they had made the hole about four feet deep, they carried the coffin from the wagon to the grave and lowered it in using ropes. Then, they covered it over with the dirt they had removed and carefully replaced the sod.

"In a week, you'd never know it had been dug up," said Lyons. "Now for the finishing touch. "Come with me, boys."

They clambered onto the wagon and drove back across the courtyard. Climbing down, they followed Lyons into a corner of the ruined cloister, where he started moving some bales of hay that had been scattered there. Hidden underneath the hay was a tarpaulin, and when Lyons pulled it back, he smiled at them and said, "The *piece de resistance!*"

Chapter 10 – London, Feb. 4

When I first moved to Baker Street in 1881, Madame Tussaud's was already a popular attraction. It was located in the Baker Street Bazaar, near Dorset Street, just a short walk from our lodgings. The founder, Madam Marie Tussaud, had died in 1850, leaving the museum to her sons. In 1883, they moved it to nearby Marylebone Road.

Family squabbles over finances caused the business to be sold in February of 1889. That was the year that Holmes and I had first met John Theodore Tussaud, Madame Tussaud's grandson, who had been retained to manage the business.

Shortly after it was sold, one of the artists who had been employed there, Edward White, was accused of sending a parcel bomb to John Theodore. Holmes was involved in the case, though he has always remained rather close-mouthed about exactly what role he played in the affair.

At any rate, I knew that we would be warmly received. And as we stepped inside, it was John Theodore himself who greeted us.

"Mr. Holmes, Dr. Watson, it has been too long. To what do I owe the honor?"

"John Theodore, how are you?" asked Holmes.

"I am well," he replied, "but unless I miss my guess, this is not a social call, is it gentlemen?"

"Would that it were," replied Holmes.

"Shall we talk in my office?" asked John Theodore.

"That would be splendid," said Holmes, and we followed our host past Lord Nelson and Sir Walter Scott as well as a number of scenes from the French Revolution.

When we had settled ourselves in his office, he rang and told the young woman who answered that he would like tea for three.

Turning his attention to us, he asked, "Now Mr. Holmes, how may I be of service?"

"You have a young woman in your employ by the name of Kathleen McMahon, do you not?" said Holmes.

"Yes, she is one of my best artists," replied John Theodore.

"Does she create the statues?" asked Holmes.

"No, Mr. Holmes," he answered, "she works in papier-mâché, and to say she is an artist is far from doing her justice."

"What exactly does she do?" asked Holmes.

"She creates the weapons that some of the figures hold as well as the backdrops against which they are posed and various other props. Wax has its limits, Mr. Holmes; even the strongest wax will soon show signs of fatigue if it is required to hold up a six-pound battle-axe all year round. However, if the axe weighs but a pound, the strain is greatly reduced and the wax will last that much longer."

"And the set pieces that she designs?"

"She has created the most realistic trees and bushes. You would swear they were real," said John Theodore.

"Anything else?" prodded Holmes.

"A great many things," replied John Theodore. "Is there something in particular you would like to know about?"

"If I needed a boulder or a large rock, could she fashion one of those?"

"I've no doubt that she could," he replied. "I say that because she has fashioned a few such stones for one of the displays."

Holmes gave me a knowing glance, and just then the woman returned with our tea.

As John Theodore served, Holmes deftly switched the topic. We made small talk about his business, and he described for us the difficulties of maintaining an audience, and dismissed as a novelty the new moving pictures that were starting to proliferate.

"Fads may come and go, but Madame Tussaud's will persevere. These moving pictures, they are but a moment long, and then they are gone. Our statues are eternal," he informed us proudly.

After we had finished, Holmes asked if we might meet with Miss McMahon. John Theodore said that he believed she was in her studio and that he would take us to her.

He led us down a darkened hall and when had he reached the end, he pulled back a deep purple curtain to reveal a door. After he had knocked, a woman's voice said, "Come in."

As we entered, I saw one of the most striking creatures I have ever encountered. I know that Holmes considers himself immune to the charms of the fairer sex; however, I am not so fortunate.

Tall and slender, Kathleen McMahon had long auburn hair, sparkling green eyes and a dazzling smile. She was standing at a workbench, painting what appeared to be a large wooden stake. Her appearance at that moment was far from flattering, as she was wearing an apron that was bespattered with daubs of various colored paint, which had also made its way onto her face and hands, Still, there was no denying the woman's obvious beauty.

"Miss McMahon, I should like to introduce Mr. Sherlock Holmes, the famous detective, and Dr. John Watson, his chronicler," said John Theodore. "Now, if you will excuse me, I have to attend to a few things elsewhere."

"I know who you are gentlemen," she replied with a slight brogue.

"You do?" I exclaimed.

"Of course," she replied.

Appraising us carefully, she said, "Two men – one quite tall with an aquiline profile and a stoic demeanor with readily apparent chemical stains on three of his fingers, who is accompanied by an obvious medical man who appears to have an injured left arm that he seems to favor slightly, I can only conclude that they must be the great detective and his Boswell."

"Well-played," said Holmes.

"Besides," she added, "I used to see you occasionally while I was out shopping, and one day I asked John Theodore, who was with me, who you might be." At that, we all laughed, and she said, "How may I help you gentlemen?"

Given a moment, I was able to survey my surroundings and looking about the room, I was stunned to see all manner of weapons – knives and swords and axes as well as shields and armor, bowls and other strange objects. Looking to my left, I saw various torture devices, including a pillory, an iron maiden and a scavenger's daughter.

"Did you create all of these?" I asked in wonderment.

"Not all, but most," she replied.

"And how long does it take you to create something like, say, a stake?" asked Holmes.

"Smaller pieces can be done in three or four days while a larger piece may require several days or more," she replied. "One has to fashion the framework from wire or wood. Then you create a mix of glue and water, although I prefer to use the paste that is employed by wallpaper hangers. It lasts much longer."

"Could you explain the process in detail?" my friend asked. "I fear it may have some bearing on a case with which I find myself involved."

"Certainly," she replied, totally unruffled. While she was speaking, Holmes busied himself prowling about the room examining her various creations. I half expected him to pull out his lens at any moment.

When she had finished a few minutes later, Holmes thanked her and said, "You have been most informative, Miss McMahon. I cannot express my gratitude."

"I'm glad I could help," she said.

"Just one more question if I may?" asked Holmes.

"Certainly," she replied.

"What part of Ireland are you from?"

"I was born and raised in the north, in Donegal," she replied.

"I thought so," replied Holmes. "I have an uncanny ear for accents. Now, let me thank you again. We will see ourselves out," Holmes said. "And please give my best to John Theodore."

"I certainly shall," she replied.

"As we left Madame Tussaud's and walked toward our lodgings, I said to Holmes, "What an absolutely captivating creature."

"That she is, Watson. However, if you are smitten, as I fear you may well be, let me caution you that Miss McMahon may find herself behind bars before this is all over, and I can't help but think that a prison sentence must certainly impede the course of true love."

Before I could say anything, Holmes said, "I am starving. Are you hungry, old man?"

Chapter 11 – Killarney, Feb. 4-5

"Where in heaven's name did you get that?" asked O'Brien.

"Remember when Santry and I went to Dublin a few weeks back? We met some of our brothers from the north – County Armagh, to be exact. On the president's orders, they had 'borrowed' this beauty from an obscure little cemetery near Greencastle."

"They transferred it from it from their wagon to ours, and here it is," Lyons explained.

"But won't it be missed?" asked Nesbitt.

"I rather doubt it," said Lyons. "Even if it is, can you imagine how many Michael Kellys must be buried in Ireland? And what better place to hide a tombstone than in a cemetery?

"Now, get those ropes and lift it carefully. It weighs about 400 pounds, Santry and I got it off the wagon with a hell of a struggle, so I think the four of us should be able to manage it without too much trouble."

And so they hoisted it into the wagon, drove back across the courtyard to the cemetery and after some exertion, managed to place it atop the grave they had just dug.

"If the English can find it here, they deserve to get it back it," said Lyons, "but I'm guessing that our secret will stay buried as long as we want it to."

"But will it not be noticed?" asked Nesbitt.

"I don't think so," said Lyons, "I told the boys the approximate date range we needed, and I told them it had to be a high cross with a common name. In other words, I have taken great pains to make certain that it fits in with its surroundings quite nicely. And as we have installed it in an older section of the cemetery, I rather doubt even the locals will notice the sudden addition."

Pausing, he looked at the men and asked, "Have I overlooked anything?"

"Not that I can think of," said Santry. "The stone blends right in and there's nothing even remotely memorable about it."

The others nodded in assent.

Feeling vindicated and a bit self-satisfied, Lyons said, "You all remember the oath you swore when you joined the Brotherhood? Then now is the time to keep your word. This is a big step in our quest to free Ireland. I know I can count on you, right?"

As he looked around, they nodded again.

Lyons then asked, "O'Brien is there anything left in that flask of yours, or have you drunk it all, you selfish bastard?"

They laughed and the bond between them was made firmer.

As they passed the whiskey, each one knew that he had played a minor role in what they were certain would be a major victory for the Irish Republican Brotherhood.

* * *

By the time they arrived home from Kerry, it was early evening. It had been a long few days, but Lyons couldn't have been happier. Things had gone smoothly, and Michael Collins had proven his worth once again.

As he drifted off to sleep, Lyons could only imagine what might have happened had Michael not begun to weep.

He woke a few hours later and was ravenously hungry. He considered cooking and decided to go to the Sin E' on Coburg Street and see what the papers had to say about the theft.

After a brisk walk of about 20 minutes, he found himself in the familiar surroundings of his favorite pub. After ordering dinner with a pint, he asked Eric if there were any newspapers about. He was rewarded with copies of the Daily Irish Independent and the Freeman's Journal. Neither had a word about the theft of the Coronation Stone.

"So that's how they want to play it," thought Lyons. "Well, two can play at that game. If they want their King to be crowned on the stone, they must make the first move."

After eating, Lyons was just about to leave the pub and head home, when Robert, the messenger from the cable office, poked his head into the door. "Oh, there you are, Mr. Lyons," he exclaimed. "I've been looking all over town for you."

"Have you now?" asked Lyons.

"This cable came in for you about an hour ago," the boy said. "I went to your house and then by the school. Then I visited Mr. Santry, and finally, I thought I'd give this place a try."

"You're a tenacious fellow," Lyons said, handing the youngster a few bob.

"Thank you, Mr. Lyons. I hope it is good news."

Opening the envelope, Lyons pulled out a single sheet of paper. It read: "Marie is doing quite well. Stop! She is visiting several homes. Stop! She may visit you next. Stop! Best, Charlotte. Stop!"

He knew it was from Kathleen because Charlotte was the code name the Brotherhood had given her in recognition of her favorite wax figure, Charlotte Corday.

He thought for a second or two doing the calculations. The first sentence had five words. The closing had two, which multiplied to 10. Counting to the tenth word, he saw "homes."

"Homes," he wondered what it might mean. However, it wasn't until he had said it aloud that the veil was suddenly lifted, It wasn't "homes" he realized, but "Holmes," and "She may visit you next" was obviously meant to convey "He may visit you next."

So, the government had brought in Sherlock Holmes, and somehow he had already found his way to Kathleen.

A few minutes later, he found himself at the telegraph office sending a reply of sorts and a second cable.

As he walked home, he thought, "Perhaps I can dissuade Sherlock Holmes from crossing the Irish Sea before he even attempts it."

He continued ruminating. "This is none of your affair, Mr. Holmes. I have no quarrel with you, but if you do have the temerity to visit me, the next adventure to run in The Strand may well be 'The Case of the Disappearing Detective'."

Chapter 12 – London, Feb. 4-5

Holmes refused to discuss Miss McMahon over dinner, so while he enjoyed his meal of trout with spinach and roasted potatoes, I could only pick at my food.

When we had finally reached our rooms and he had settled into his chair with his pipe, I broached the subject of Miss McMahon once again.

"Watson, had you taken less notice of her smile and paid more attention to her workroom, you would not begrudge me my suspicions.

"To begin with, did you see all the chicken wire that she uses to make her frameworks? It is the exact same type that was used to construct the counterfeit stone."

"You yourself said it was of the most common type," I replied.

"Indeed, I did," Holmes admitted. "But there is also the matter of the paint. She has the same three colors in her studio that were used to create the substitute."

"And many others as well. Again, you said the paint was very common. It could just be a coincidence," I said.

"You said that to me once before old friend, do you recall?"

"Honestly, no," I replied.

"In the case that you dubbed 'The Adventure of the Second Stain,' I intended to interview a man named Eduardo Lucas, and you informed me that he had been killed the previous night. When I asked your opinion, you called it 'an amazing coincidence.' Again, Watson, she has the wire, she has the paint, and, more important, she has the skill to execute such a task. I tell you now as I did then: The odds are enormous against its being coincidence. No figures could express them.

"And if all that weren't enough," he continued, "were you to examine the manner in which the papier-mâché has been trimmed on certain sections of the stone and compare it to the way that Miss O'Brien has trimmed her creations, you would find that they are very similar – if not identical.

"She is involved, Watson. Whether she is a willing participant or has been coerced remains to be seen. Given your obvious fondness for her, I can only hope it is the latter. Still, for right now, she is the best lead that we have and her actions will require careful scrutiny."

Although I was shattered, I knew that my friend was correct. Sometimes, I could find his logic infuriating.

The next morning when I awoke, Holmes was gone. When Mrs. Hudson brought me my breakfast, she informed me that Holmes had left the house quite early.

I spent much of the day reading the papers and catching up on my correspondence. When I had finished my writing, I was surprised to see that it was late afternoon, and I still had not heard from my friend.

Although Holmes had a history of disappearing from time to time, he usually would keep me informed, so I was just beginning to worry when I heard his familiar footsteps on the stair.

When he entered I could see that his face was flushed and his right hand was wrapped in a handkerchief as though he had injured it. Despite his rather disheveled appearance, his air was decidedly jubilant.

Looking at him, I said, "Holmes, what have you been up to?"

He smiled broadly and said, "I was just set upon by two blackguards in the street."

"You're joking," I exclaimed.

"I assure you Watson, I am not. There are two proud sons of Erin who will bear witness to my story."

"You know who they were?" I asked.

"I do not know their names, but I can certainly find them should the need arise."

"And they were Irish?"

"Indeed," said Holmes. "Both had heavy brogues. As I turned onto Baker Street from Allsop Place, I noticed the two of them loitering right in front of our door, so I walked right past them onto Melcombe Street and then to Glentworth Street. I then walked along to Ivor Place and then to Park Road and so made my way back to Baker. They were still there – just standing and waiting. But now I knew that they were waiting for me even though they did not know me.

"Having gained the upper hand, I walked up to them and said, 'I am Sherlock Holmes. I can see that you have been waiting for me for quite some time. How may I be of assistance?'

"To say that they were taken aback would be something of an understatement," Holmes said as he examined his bruised and bloody knuckles.

"Let me get my bag," I said.

"There's really no need," Holmes continued.

Feeling his hand, I could tell that none of the bones had been broken, but he did have two rather nasty cuts. "Just let me clean and bandage these," I said, fetching my satchel.

While I was tending to Holmes' hand, he continued his story.

"After they had recovered, one of them said, 'Mr. Holmes, I have been asked to deliver a message to you.'

"Have you?" I asked. "And what would that be?"

"Pulling a paper from his pocket, he read, 'This is one stone you must leave unturned or face the consequences.'

"Are you threatening me?" I asked.

"Take it any way you like," said the first one, "but you have been warned.

"At that point, the second one decided to insert himself into the conversation. 'We do not threaten, Mr. Holmes. We promise.'

"And exactly what is it that you are promising?"

"'Pain'," he said, "'such as you have never felt.' At that point, he attempted to shove me, but as he went to extend his arms, I sidestepped, grabbed his wrist and twisted it so hard that he screamed.

"'Like that?' I asked. And then it was on. The first one then attempted to punch me, but he missed, so I hit him as hard as I could in the face. I may have knocked a tooth or two loose – and hurt my hand in the process. By now, the second one had recovered to a degree, and he made a feeble attempt to strike me in the head with his other hand.

"I blocked that blow, and hit him squarely in the nose with the same hand I had used on his companion."

As they lie on the ground, I said, "Tell whoever sent you that he must do better next time."

"You let them go," I exclaimed.

"I did, but as I said, I can find them should the need arise."

"Did you try to follow them?"

"No," said Holmes. "There was really no need. Besides, they had given me plenty of information already."

"In that warning?" I asked.

"No," replied Holmes, holding up a piece of foolscap, "In this note that the first one was kind enough to drop during our slight set-to.

"By the way, Watson, I am attacked by a pair of Irish toughs the day after we visit your Miss McMahon. Do you think that a coincidence as well?"

Holmes can be absolutely maddening when he is correct.

Chapter 13 – London, Feb. 6

Kathleen had always known the day might come when she would be forced to abandon her comfortable London life.

She had just never imagined that it would arrive this soon.

The ironic part was, she thought, that she had committed no crime. All she had done was accept a commission from an old friend to create a papier-mâché replica of the Stone of Destiny.

She was pretty certain that although it might eventually be traced to her, there would be the devil to pay before they could prove that she had actually fashioned it.

All the materials used had been of the most common types. Still, as she packed, she wondered how Holmes had tumbled so quickly to the fact that it was she who had fashioned it. She had watched him prowl about her workroom, picking up some of her creations and examining others quite closely, all with an air of practiced nonchalance, and the entire time he continued to feign interest in her discussion of the papier-mâché process.

She had to admit his performance had been quite good, but she had seen right through his little charade. When she heard that Holmes had bested the two men Lyons had sent to frighten him, she had known that it was time to return home.

Besides, she missed her family, and she knew that they had missed her as well.

After she had carried her bag downstairs and bid her landlord farewell, she hired a cab to take her to the new Marylebone terminus of the Great Central Railway. There was a train leaving for Liverpool at 11 a.m., and she was determined to be on it, then across the sea and she would be home in Clonakilty by tomorrow.

When she arrived at the station, she purchased her ticket and saw that she had a little less than an hour until her departure. With nothing else to do, she set out to explore the station and its amenities.

She was so engrossed in her thoughts that it was quite a few minutes before she thought that a young boy, no more than 11 or 12, had been following her throughout the station.

Thinking that the youngster might be one of Holmes' legendary street urchins, she determined to confront the lad, but when she wheeled around to accuse him, there was no one there.

Although she felt relieved, she was determined not to let her guard down again.

When she boarded the train, she felt a definite sense of relief. She had not seen the youngster again, nor had anyone else aroused her suspicions. She might miss London, she thought, but she knew that she would be far happier – and of much greater use to the cause – in Ireland.

Chapter 14 – London, Feb. 6

Late the next morning, Holmes and I once again received an urgent summons to the Diogenes Club. As we were leaving our lodgings, a young boy ran up to Holmes, and after catching his breath, the youngster handed my friend a note.

After reading it, Holmes said, "You have done well, John." Then he wrote a short note, fished a few quid from his pocket, and said, "Give these to Dicky when you see him. Tell him to be careful and to keep in touch."

The youngster looked at the money with eyes as big as saucers, then he snapped to attention, saluted and said, "I will, Mr. Holmes," and then he scampered off.

"Pray tell, what was all that about?" I asked.

"In due time, Watson," replied Holmes and then he lapsed into thought.

When we arrived at the Diogenes Club, we found Mycroft waiting for us in the Stranger's Room.

"This must be a matter of some import to disrupt your daily routine," said Holmes.

"Despite our best efforts, we have not been able to recover the stone," said Mycroft. "Quite frankly, we have no idea where it might be," he said bitterly.

"Well, I think we can safely assume that it is no longer in England," said Holmes.

"I quite agree," said Mycroft. "If it were, between your contacts and mine, I am certain that we should have heard some rumblings as to its location."

"Well, I do have one promising avenue of inquiry," said Holmes, who then proceeded to inform Mycroft in painstaking detail about his investigations into the papier-mâché artists, concluding with the attack by the two thugs the previous evening.

When he had finished, Mycroft said, "I shall put Miss McMahon under constant surveillance. Perhaps she will make a misstep of some sort."

"I fear she is far too clever for that," said Holmes. "I am also afraid that you are too late."

Taking out his watch, he looked at it and said, "Unless they are running late, Miss McMahon boarded a train bound for Liverpool thirty-seven minutes ago."

"The boy!" I exclaimed.

Holmes smiled, "I have had my lads keeping an eye on her since shortly after our first meeting. Late last night, she received a telegram, and this morning she departed London. I think it is safe to say that our fair Miss McMahon is returning home."

"Well played," said Mycroft.

Holmes smiled and said, "And unless my ears deceive me, she is headed to County Cork – not Donegal."

"We must resolve this with all due haste," said Mycroft.

"I shall do my best," replied Holmes, "but at this point, the matter is almost entirely out of our hands. We can only react to their next move. So we must wait for them to take action, and hope that we are given a clearer sense of purpose and direction."

Pausing, he looked at Mycroft, and said simply, "Out with it. Why this sudden sense of urgency?"

Mycroft looked at us and then he actually stuck his head into the hall to see if anyone were in the vicinity. Since members of the Diogenes Club are not allowed to take notice of one another, I could only assume that Mycroft was willing to risk this serious breach of club etiquette because of the gravity of the situation.

Turning back to us, he stated, "The Prime Minister has informed me that King Edward refuses to be crowned until the Coronation Stone has been recovered. Obviously, the coronation will not take place until after a suitable period of mourning has passed."

"So then time is on our side," said Holmes.

"It would seem so," said Mycroft. "Still, there appears to be no negotiating with him on that point. Although he rules the Empire, he has made it quite clear that he wants order restored as soon as possible. He has sworn that he will not even entertain the notion of accepting the crown in Westminster until the stone is once again a part of the Coronation Chair."

I hardly expected Holmes to react in the manner in which he did.

"You can't be serious," he said to Mycroft. "He doesn't believe all the myths and legends associated with the stone, does he?"

"I am not privy to the workings of the King's mind," said Mycroft. "Although if I were required to explain His Majesty's motives, I would ascribe them to the manner in which he thinks family members might react to a coronation taking place under anything less than ideal circumstances.

"I should also think tradition plays a large role in this. Just as it is difficult for us to imagine a coronation without the Crown Jewels, I think His Majesty feels that way about the Coronation Stone. He wants everything in its proper place before he will even consider planning his coronation."

"Yes, I should think you are on the right track there," said Holmes. "Fortunately, that appears to buy us a bit of time."

"In the interim," Mycroft said, "all I can do is relay the message which I received from Downing Street. His Majesty will not even consider accepting the crown until the stone has been recovered."

"And you have been tasked with the recovery?" asked Holmes.

Mycroft merely shrugged.

"So now your task has become my burden," Holmes continued. "I will get to the bottom of this," said my friend, "and I will do it in as expedient a manner as is possible. However, I do have certain conditions."

"I would have expected nothing less," said Mycroft.

"I will brook no interference from the local constabulary – either here or in Ireland," said Holmes, "and if I should require something of you, it will be provided with no questions asked."

"Within reason," said Mycroft.

"That point is not negotiable," said Holmes.

"Done," said Mycroft with a hint of resignation.

"One final thing," said Holmes. "I shall be reimbursed for any expenses incurred."

"Of course," said Mycroft, "I'm surprised you thought you had to ask."

"I have found that it is always better to leave nothing to chance," Holmes said. "Now, if you will excuse us, we have a King to comfort."

"And you will keep me informed?" asked Mycroft.

"I fear that my reports may be irregular, but to the extent that I am able, I shall endeavor to keep you abreast of our progress."

When we had departed, I said to Holmes, "So you have a plan?"

"I have a very definite idea of how to proceed, Watson," he said. During the ride back to Baker Street, he explained his proposed course of action to me.

When he had finished, I said, "You are playing a very dangerous game."

"I quite agree," he replied, "but I fear I have no other choice."

Chapter 15 – Feb. 7

After a fairly calm voyage across the Irish Sea aboard the Prince of Wales, Kathleen made her way to disembark and saw Lyons waiting on the pier for her.

As she reached the bottom of the gangplank, he embraced her and said, "Welcome home, my girl. You've done well."

"I've done what had to be done," she said resolutely. "The cause is all that matters."

Once they had put her bags into his carriage, they began to drive to her home. They hadn't gone very far before Lyons asked, "Have you any idea how Holmes tumbled to you so quickly?"

"Oh, he's a sharp customer that Mr. Sherlock Holmes. I cannot say for certain, but I should think that my reputation as a papier-mâché artist is what brought him to Madame Tussaud's."

"Yes, I should have anticipated that," admitted Lyons.

"You should have seen him," continued Kathleen. "He was skulking about my workroom, touching everything, examining each item very carefully – all the while looking for clues while pretending to listen to me."

"Did he find any?" asked Lyons.

"I do not think so, but I cannot say for certain. All I know is that had I remained there, a single slip on my part and we might all have been undone."

"No, coming home was the right decision. We have other eyes and ears in London. None quite as sharp as yours – or as pretty Miss Donnelly," said Lyons. "By the way, why did you change your name?"

"When you first broached this scheme a few years back, I decided that if your grand plan should ever come to fruition, which it has, the fewer loose ends the better. So Kathleen Donnelly set sail on the Tynwald in Cobh that day, and Kathleen McMahon disembarked in Liverpool. If Mr. Sherlock Holmes should come to Ireland, he will waste his time searching for a Kathleen McMahon who no longer exists. And, best of all, he'll be looking in Donegal and other points north, not here in Cork."

Lyons laughed. "You are truly amazing," he exclaimed, adding, "I wonder how many times Mr. Holmes has been bested. Not too many, I'm sure of that. But you have done it, Kathleen, and lived to tell the tale."

"Yes, but there's no tale to tell unless Ireland is free," she said. "Have you sent the telegram?"

"Some of the boys up north are going to send it from Dublin," he replied.

"And you trust them?"

"You know that we all take an oath of secrecy when we join the Brotherhood," he said. "I would trust those men with my life, just as I would trust you."

"And what will it say?"

"It's very direct and to the point," he said. "It says simply:
> 'If Edward would be crowned on the stone,
> Then Ireland must be free'."

"That's a lovely sentiment," she said. "Do you think they will accept it?

"Honestly, I don't know," replied Lyons. "I suppose it all depends on how important the stone is to King Edward. If he wants it returned, then he must agree to our terms. If he does not, then the stone can remain exactly where it is, and the press will soon learn that it has been taken. Perhaps that revelation will sway public opinion to our side."

"And it may just as easily turn the people against us," she said.

"You're right, of course. However, that is a chance I'm not only willing to take, but one that I feel I must. The British are celebrating a hundred years of Irish domination – an entire century. That's far too long, and I say it must end now. It has to end now!"

He had grown quite passionate during his little speech, and Kathleen could see why he was so effective as a schoolmaster and why he had risen through the ranks of the

Brotherhood so rapidly. Denis Lyons was a natural-born leader who challenged others to be better and who pushed himself as hard, if not harder, than he pushed them.

For the first time, she began to think that perhaps they had a real chance for success.

And then Lyons concluded, "And if they do not agree, I have other plans that may be employed to bring pressure on the throne. I pray that they are not necessary."

"What are you thinking?"

"If it comes to that, you shall know soon enough. I just pray that it never does."

They lapsed into a prolonged silence and then all of a sudden Kathleen's thoughts were interrupted by a voice yelling, "It's Kathleen! She's come home, Ma." And she looked up to see her brother Frank, standing in front of their cottage, waving to her excitedly even as her mother's face appeared in the doorway.

"We have a good life," she thought as the carriage stopped in front of the home. "I just hope that my actions are not the cause of misery for my family and my country."

And then she climbed down to her mother's embrace and all thoughts of the possible conflict were eclipsed by the joy at being reunited with her family. "If only Da were alive," she thought, "my happiness would be complete."

But at the same time, the thoughts of her father's death steeled her resolve. Caught somewhere between joy and determination, Kathleen Donnelly, late of Madame Tussaud's in London, was a woman in conflict.

Chapter 16 – London, Feb. 8

The next morning Holmes and I breakfasted together, and we reviewed and made a few slight revisions to his plan.

I was filled with doubts about being able to hold up my end, but Holmes kept reassuring me that I had nothing to worry about.

"I am not nearly so deft a dissembler as you," I said.

"That's because you haven't practiced as much as I have," he explained. "Once you come to believe in your new self, I should think you will find it comes naturally to you, Watson."

I sniffed, "I suppose that was intended as a compliment of some sort."

"Indeed it was," exclaimed Holmes. "Now, let us go visit Oliver and see what suggestions he may offer. I have some thoughts of my own, but I am always eager to get the opinion of a professional in these matters – especially when it doesn't concern me."

"Are you certain this is really necessary?"

"It is absolutely imperative," said Holmes, "I'm going to ask you to play a much larger role in this case than is normally your wont."

"You can rely on me," I said.

We hailed a cab and headed for the East End. I knew that Holmes had many friends who worked in the theater. While some were performers, others served in a variety of functions, from stage managers such as Bram Stoker, to makeup artists such as Oliver Kennedy.

One of his oldest and dearest friends, Kennedy was a gentle giant of a man, who also served as the wardrobe manager and jack-of-all-trades at the St. James Theatre on King Street. I had never met Kennedy, but I knew that Holmes trusted him and had relied on him on several occasions in the past.

The theater was empty when we arrived. Thankfully, the stage door had been left open, and soon Holmes and I were standing on the proscenium. Thinking back, I recalled spending many pleasurable nights here watching such triumphs as "Lady Windermere's Fan" and the premiere of "The Importance of Being Ernest," both by Oscar Wilde. The latter had been staged shortly before his precipitous fall from grace and imprisonment. I had also enjoyed Anthony Hope's swashbuckler, "The Prisoner of Zenda."

One of the most storied theatres in all of London, the St. James also boasted in its history that a young Charles Dickens had trod the boards there in 1846, appearing as Captain Bobadil in an amateur performance of Ben Jonson's "Every Man in His Humor."

Standing there, I was roused from my thoughts by a booming voice exclaiming, "Mr. Holmes, it is so good to see you again."

Oliver Kennedy emerged from the side of the stage and greeted us warmly. After Holmes had introduced me, Kennedy said, "So I have you to thank for chronicling all of our friend's adventures. I am in your debt, sir."

I expressed my appreciation for his kind words, and then he turned to Holmes and said, "How may I be of assistance?"

Holmes then outlined what he hoped Kennedy might accomplish and concluded by saying, "As you know, I can fend for myself in this department. It is Dr. Watson's safety that is of paramount concern here. Do you think you can help us?"

"I don't see why not," said Kennedy jovially. "Besides, I do appreciate a good challenge."

"Follow me," said Kennedy as he led us backstage. Taking us into a well-lit room, he had me sit in front of a large mirror. Cupping his chin in his hand, Kennedy began to study me. After making a full circle around me and analyzing me from every possible angle, he said, "I think I have it."

I was almost afraid to hear what he was thinking, but I finally mustered up the courage to ask, "What is it that you think you have?"

"The first thing we must do is shave the moustache," he announced.

I do not consider myself a vain man, but this seemed to me totally unnecessary. "Can't we just trim it a bit?" I asked.

"Out of the question, Doctor," said Kennedy. "Next, we cut the hair differently – much shorter – and dye it gray. Finally, we give you a limp, perhaps a cane, and possibly spectacles. Top it off with a new wardrobe and Dr. John Watson is no more. In his place, we have...," he let the words trail off and looked at Holmes.

Studying me and envisioning Kennedy's suggested alterations to my appearance, Holmes finished the sentence, "... Sgt. George Ward, late of the 10th Royal Hussars, wounded at the Battle of Maiwand. Now working as a stevedore."

Holmes explained, "You always want there to be an element of truth in the lie you tell. There is simply no way to conceal that you were once a military man, so we must take that into account and include it as part of your new identity.

"Now, I will leave you in Mr. Kennedy's capable hands, and I shall return in..." he looked at Kennedy.

"Give me an hour or so, Mr. Holmes," said Kennedy.

Holmes looked at me, "I bid you farewell for the moment, Dr. Watson. I shall see you anon – or perhaps not you, exactly."

After Holmes left, Kennedy led me into another room and bade me sit down. He then began to shave my moustache and then he cut and dyed my hair. All the while, he refused to allow me to see a mirror. After asking my shoe size, he brought me a pair of boots, and in the left one he placed a small heel-shaped wedge.

"That may be uncomfortable for a while," he explained, "but it changes your balance just enough to throw it off and makes you walk with a very slight but obvious limp."

"Try it," he encouraged.

Pulling the boots on after adjusting the wedge, I tried to stride across the room, but I found myself walking a bit slower than I might have normally and taking extra careful steps with my left foot.

"You see," he exclaimed, "I know you didn't believe me, but now you do."

He then spun around and reached into a closet. Turning back to me, he handed me several more wedges. "These are all different heights," he explained. "If you feel yourself getting too comfortable, simply change the one in the boot for one of these and your limp will miraculously reappear.

"Now," he said, thinking aloud, "the clothes." He looked me up and down and then said, "I shall return momentarily."

He came back a few minutes later with a pile of garments. Handing me a well-worn pair of gray gabardine trousers, he urged, "Try these on."

I pulled my trousers off and the ones he had handed me on. The waist was just about right, but the legs were far too long.

Reaching into his vest pocket, he pulled out a piece of tailor's chalk and quickly marked them. "Give them to me," he said, "I'll return shortly."

When he reappeared a moment later, he handed me a dark blue cambric shirt and a heavy, wool pea coat. He had a good eye because both fit reasonably well. Finally, I was given a knitted watch cap, which I pulled on my head.

"Just so you know doctor, that is a very special cap," he said.

"How so?" I asked.

"It is double-lined. Can you feel that?"

Pulling it off my head, I looked inside and saw that he was telling the truth.

"There are lots of double-lined caps," I said. "What's so unusual about this one?"

"Indeed, there are," he replied. "But not all double-lined caps will do double-duty as a balaclava. I have no idea what you and Mr. Holmes are about, but there it is, should you need it. I will give you an extra one for Mr. Holmes – just in case."

At that moment, there was a knock at the door and Kennedy answered it and returned with my trousers. After I had pulled them on along with the boots, I stood up and looked at him. "I must say, I feel ridiculous. I can't imagine how silly I must appear."

"Well then, you must have a look at yourself," said Kennedy. "But before you do, one last thing."

He walked over and opened a drawer. Taking out a tray filled with spectacles, he chose a silver pair and said, "Try these on. The lenses are just glass, so they will not affect your vision."

Gazing at me once more, he said, "Follow me."

We walked back to the room where we had begun, and he said, "Now, you may take a look."

I must admit that when I saw my reflection, I was stunned. I looked like a worker who had spent too many rough years on the waterfront. If clothes make the man, rest assured, they can also unmake him. To say that I looked disreputable would be doing Kennedy a disservice. I thought that I appeared positively….

"Yes, Watson, you do look rather dangerous," said Holmes, who had entered the room. "Oliver, you have done splendidly. I believe his own mother wouldn't recognize him."

"Thank you, Mr. Holmes. I am happy to be of service."

"I won't bother to ask how you knew what I was thinking," I said. "I've seen that trick before."

As we were about to depart, Kennedy said, "Wait here just one moment."

When he returned a few minutes later, he was carrying a package wrapped in brown paper, which he handed to me.

"What on Earth?" I sputtered.

"Some extra clothes," he explained, "Even the most weathered laborer has a spare pair of trousers and more than one shirt. Your own clothes are in there as well."

As we left, Holmes tried to slip Kennedy some notes, but he was having none of it. "Think of it as payment in part for the many favors that you have done me," Kennedy said. "Good luck, gentlemen. If I can be of further assistance, you know where to find me."

"Now, we shall put your disguise to the test, Watson. If you are able to deceive Mrs. Hudson, I should think you might fool anyone."

Holmes stopped the cab a few blocks before our lodgings. He told me to walk to Baker Street, and he would go on ahead and tell Mrs. Hudson that he was expecting a caller shortly.

As I limped along Baker Street, I was grateful for the warm clothes, Kennedy had provided me. Having no gloves, I had to thrust my hands deep into my pockets.

After about ten minutes, I arrived at 221B and rang the bell. Fearing that Mrs. Hudson might recognize my voice, I tried to speak more slowly than I normally do, and I also tried to speak from the back of my throat.

I heard myself say, "I am here to see Mr. Sherlock Holmes."

After thoroughly appraising me, Mrs. Hudson said simply, "Wait here." Then she abruptly closed the door in my face.

She opened it a few moments later and said brusquely, "Mr. Holmes will see you now."

I followed her up the stairs and she led me into our rooms.

"It's so good to see you," said Holmes warmly.

As Mrs. Hudson started to leave, Holmes said, "Mrs. Hudson, would you bring me a cup of tea?" Pausing, he added, "And Watson, would you care for one as well?"

Turning around, Mrs. Hudson glanced at my bedroom door, but then realizing there was no one else in the room, she began to look at me again.

Finally, she came closer and after examining me very carefully, she turned to my friend and said, "Mr. Holmes, I am used to you playing dress-up, but now you have Dr. Watson doing it too." With that, she shook her head and left.

After she had departed, Holmes said, "She will be your toughest critic. If you stay in character, I am certain that you can deceive Miss McMahon if you should happen to encounter her on the streets of Cork."

"Do you think that likely?"

"I do not know, but I am loath to take any chances with your safety," said Holmes.

I must admit that I was genuinely touched by my friend's expression of concern.

Chapter 17 – London, Feb. 8-11

After Mrs. Hudson had brought us the tea and departed, Holmes said, "I received another communiqué from Mycroft.

"He informs me that the government has received a telegram saying the stone will be returned when Ireland is free. As you might expect, that makes our task considerably more difficult.

"Right now, the only thing we know is the stone is probably in Ireland. We do not yet know how it was transported there, although I have developed a theory.

"That said, our only lead of substance is one Miss Kathleen McMahon, late of Madame Tussaud's. With regard to said Miss McMahon, we know that she is a skilled papier-mâché artist. I am reasonably certain that she comes from County Cork, her protestations about Donegal notwithstanding.

"We also know that at present Cork is the largest county in Ireland, with a population of some 350,000 souls. It is incredibly diverse in that it contains both Protestants and Catholics. Of more interest to us is the fact that in Cork can be found a unionist community, which favors the status quo between Britain and Ireland; a nationalist majority, whose leanings are diametrically opposed; and a small contingent of radical republicans, who are the wild cards in this deck.

"If I were a betting man, I would give you odds that we will find our quarry among the last group."

"Can we count on any of the others to help us?" I asked.

"I do not know," said Holmes. "I am pretty certain that we will be able to find allies among the unionists, but who they are and how trustworthy they may be – that remains to be seen.

"Now, a few more things about your character, Sgt. Ward. The observant will notice your hands are rather soft. They lack the callouses that a real laborer would have developed. To help conceal that fact, I stopped at Harrods and purchased a pair of fingerless leather gloves. You must wear them at all times, and I know this will pain you, but you must also try to keep your hands as dirty as possible."

"I understand," I said, though I must admit I was rather repulsed by the thought of not being able to wash my hands as frequently as I liked.

"Anything else?" I wondered.

"I think it would help if you shaved but once a week."

"And?" I continued.

"Your manners must go on holiday," suggested Holmes. "Consider the station of your character, not your own, A laborer would rather spend his money on drink than handkerchiefs. To that end, you might keep a small flask in your pocket."

"Holmes, is there anything you haven't thought of?" I asked.

"I hope not, Watson," said Holmes turning quite serious. "Any oversight on my part or slip-up on yours might mean our lives, and I should never forgive myself if something were to happen to you."

"We've been down this road many times," I said. "This is just one more excursion."

Little did I know how wrong I would be.

The next morning, Holmes and I dined together and went over our plans one more time.

Holmes was to leave that night, and I was to follow him in three days' time. He would find lodgings and send a telegram to the main post office in Cork for George Ward, instructing me where and when to meet him.

The day seemed to drag out endlessly. Finally, around 5 p.m., Holmes emerged from his room dressed as a chimney sweep. His clothes were disheveled and his sooty face and hands bore mute testament to his occupation.

He was carrying a bag filled with brushes and other tools, including a rather evil looking borer.

Although I knew it was Holmes, the face was somehow different. He also appeared shorter and stockier, and when he finally spoke it was with a heavy brogue. I will not try to duplicate it here, but you may rest assured that Holmes was impeccable in his cadence and inflections.

Looking at me he said, "I'm off Watson, I shall look for you in three days. While I am gone, stay in character. Go to the docks and listen to the voices and the slang the workers use. It is not genteel, but it is authentic."

With that he headed for the door, as he opened it, he said to me, "Watson?"

"Yes," I replied without thinking.

"That could have been a costly misstep," he cautioned. "For the foreseeable future, Dr. John Watson is no more."

I said, "That wasn't quite fair."

He replied, "I do not think the people we are up against are overly concerned with the niceties of rules or fairness."

Although it pained me, I had to admit that once again Holmes had been right, and I was determined not to disappoint my friend a second time.

I did as Holmes suggested and devoted the next three days to honing my character. I spent most of my time down on the wharfs by the Thames, watching the way sailors and longshoremen walked and talked and joked with one another.

It helped with a number of little things such as inflections and colloquialisms. It also allowed me to catch myself on a couple of occasions. One time I entered a shop and was about to buy the Times. Seeing my reflection in the mirror behind the counter, I realized Sgt. Ward would not be reading that particular paper, so at the last minute, I asked for a pack of cigarettes instead.

On the morning of the fourth day, I left our rooms and again caught myself. Instead of hailing a cab, I limped a few blocks, carrying my bag, and boarded a horse-drawn bus for Paddington Station.

I thought I was getting fairly comfortable in my character, and I was certain that Holmes would be pleased.

Instead of a compartment, I purchased an ordinary coach ticket and soon found myself in a cramped carriage, filled with people from all walks of life.

With no book to read and no Holmes to talk to, I quickly nodded off and was awakened when we pulled into Birmingham. The car let off more people than it took on, so there was a bit more room to stretch out. Someone had left a copy of the Daily Mail on the seat next to me.

The Daily Mail had been started just a few years earlier by the Harmsworth brothers, both of whom were viscounts. I thought the paper, being so new, had little cachet and even though it was aimed at the middle-class, I believed it to be the type of paper Sgt. Ward might read. It helped pass the time and there were several articles that I thought Holmes might find interesting, so I tried to commit them to memory. After I had dozed off for a second time, I awoke as the train jerked to a stop in the Liverpool station.

I made my way to the waterfront and booked passage to Cork and soon found myself wishing I had held onto the paper. Although I was able to purchase a cup of tea and a meal on the boat, I realized that I should have eaten a bigger breakfast. By the time we left Dublin, I was famished and couldn't wait to dock and get something substantial under my belt.

I arrived in Cobh long after dinner time. With no idea of where I was to stay or when I would see Holmes, I decided that food was my first priority. Remembering my station in life,

I asked one of the deckhands, rather than a steward, where I might get something to eat.

He suggested I take a horse-drawn bus train into Cork City and recommended several pubs, his favorite being The Cottage Inn on Curragh Road. After about a 40-minute ride, I found myself standing in front of the pub. Venturing inside, I discovered it was filled with all manner of working-class people.

After a meal of shepherd's pie, which was quite tasty, and an ale, I asked my serving girl for directions to the main telegraph office. She told me it was about a 25-minute walk to Oliver Plunkett Street. She also told me the post office was closed but that the telegraph office there was open all night.

After my trek, I entered the telegraph office on Plunkett Street and asked a young woman if they might be holding any wires for Sgt. George Ward. She returned a minute later and handed me an envelope.

I signed for it, opened it and read, "Careful. Stop. The vicar is coming. Stop."

Holmes and I had prearranged a code. The seven letters in the first sentence gave me the house number and the use of the word vicar gave me the name of the thoroughfare. Finally, the six-letter word "coming" told me it was Vicar Street. Had the vicar been right or away, it would have been Vicar Road or avenue.

After leaving the post office, I asked a young mother with three children how to get to Vicar Street. She said it was about a 15-minute walk from Tuckey to South Main Street and then across the River Lee where South Main would become Barrack Street, which would lead me directly to Vicar on my right.

The thought of seeing Holmes again quickened my walk and scarcely 10 minutes later, I found myself knocking on the door of 7 Vicar Street.

A voice from within said, "Come inside and close the door directly."

Chapter 18 – Clonakilty, Feb. 12-13

Denis Lyons was growing impatient. He had sent the telegram to the British government five days ago, and there had been no reaction. It was as though the King and Prime Minister had decided to pretend that nothing was amiss. The only small comfort he could take was the fact that nothing about the coronation had been announced either, so perhaps they were waiting for him to make the next move.

Analyzing the situation, Lyons thought, the British had time on their side, but he had the stone. Reasoning that an impasse would serve no one, he determined to press the issue.

Going to the school where he taught, he decided to compose a letter explaining exactly what would happen if there were no signs of progress in the immediate future.

Sitting alone, he began to write. After a number of stops and starts and several revisions, he finally arrived at a message that he thought would convey a strong sense of purpose and, with the addition of a small token, would drive home his point in a manner that could not be missed.

As he re-read the letter once again, he was struck by the distinctiveness of his handwriting. At that point, he decided that he would type the letter on the headmaster's new typewriter. "That way it can never be traced back to me," he thought.

He had considered the school foolish when it decided to spend so much money on a machine – money he felt might have been better used for books, but as he entered the headmaster's office to begin typing, he was glad, for the moment, that they had ignored his protestations.

Hitting each key very carefully and slowly, he began:

YOUR ROYAL MAJESTY,

PLEASE ACCEPT OUR DEEPEST CONDOLENCES ON THE PASSING OF YOUR MOTHER.

HOWEVER, THERE IS OTHER BUSINESS THAT REQUIRES YOUR IMMEDIATE ATTENTION.

AS I AM SURE YOU KNOW BY NOW, THE STONE OF DESTINY, OR THE CORONATION STONE, IS NO LONGER IN YOUR POSSESSION. SHOULD YOU WISH TO ADHERE TO CENTURIES OF TRADITION AND ACCEPT YOUR CROWN WHILE SITTING ON THE CORONATION CHAIR IN WESTMINSTER ABBEY, THEN YOU MUST GRANT IRELAND ITS FREEDOM. FOR TOO LONG, WE HAVE GROANED UNDER THE YOKE OF YOUR TYRANNY.

IF, HOWEVER, THE CUSTOMS OF YOUR ANCESTORS MEAN LITTLE TO YOU, THEN YOU MAY TAKE THE CROWN TOMORROW.

JUST SO THAT YOU WILL NOT BE TOTALLY BEREFT OF YOUR TRADITIONS, I HAVE ENCLOSED A SMALL PIECE OF THE STONE UPON WHICH YOU MAY FEEL FREE TO SIT.

THERE WILL BE NO NEGOTIATING.

IRELAND WILL BE FREE OR THE STONE OF
DESTINY WILL FIND A RESTING PLACE IN THE
BOTTOM OF A BOG, FAR FROM YOUR HANDS.

BRAITHREACHAS PHOBLACHT NA HEIREANN

THE IRISH REPUBLICAN BROTHERHOOD

After he had read it over several times, he typed a
second copy. He then went home and slept, knowing that he
had a hard ride ahead of him the next day.

Rising very early, he set out before daybreak for
County Tipperary. He knew that he could not send the parcel
without O'Leary's authorization.

As he rode through the beautiful Gaelic countryside, he
thought about the centuries of injustices that had been heaped
upon his nation by England.

And then he considered the struggle for freedom.
Whoever had first organized the Brotherhood had done a
masterful job. All of the top members were protected by layers
of secrecy. In fact, he was one of only nine men who knew that
John O'Leary, whom he was going to see, was the president of
the Brotherhood. In turn, only nine men knew that he was an
officer.

Lately, though, he had come to believe that tongues
were wagging in certain quarters, but that was a subject that he
and his eight counterparts would have to take up with O'Leary
another day.

He thought about England celebrating the centenary of the Act of Union, and he considered how the British had bribed their way to having it passed in the Irish Parliament.

Since that time, no Catholic in Ireland had been truly free, and the bitter taste of subjugation rose in Lyons' throat.

He passed the hours thinking about the history of the struggle and the great sacrifices made by those who had come before him and loved freedom as much as he did.

It was early evening when he finally arrived at the farm of John McGettigan. To say that his counterpart in Tipperary was taken aback to see him would be an understatement.

"Denis, what brings you this way?" asked McGettigan.

"I'll be needing a word with Himself," replied Lyons.

"I'll send one of my boys to fetch him," McGettigan said, "In the meantime, come inside and refresh yourself. You'll be staying for dinner, and I'll have Margaret make up the extra bedroom for you."

McGettigan called his eldest son, Robert, and said, "Tell Mr. O'Leary, if he is free, that we should like to meet with him here tonight. Tell him it is important, and we have a visitor from Clonakilty."

While Robert was gone, Lyons and McGettigan sat at the table, talking about the movement. Margaret McGettigan brought them plates of beef stew and brown bread along with a pitcher of hard cider.

Just as they were finishing, Robert returned and said, "Mr. O'Leary says he will be here at ten o'clock."

"That's a good lad," McGettigan said, "Now run along and eat before your mother yells at me."

After the boy left, McGettigan said, "So tell me about your adventure in London."

For the next hour, Lyons recounted the tale of the theft for his host.

When he had finished, McGettigan said, "So where do things stand now?"

At that moment, there was a knock on the door, and before McGettigan could rise to answer it, John O'Leary had let himself in.

Looking more like a scholar, which he was, than a firebrand, O'Leary said, "It's good to see you, John, and Denis, what can I say? If the country knew what you had done, there would be a statue erected in your honor in every freedom-loving town."

"You flatter me," said Denis. "But it's that business that brings me here."

"Go on," said O'Leary.

"There has been no response to the first telegram, so I composed a second letter. I wanted you to read it and see if you thought it hit the right tone."

Pulling a paper from his pocket, he handed it to O'Leary, who perused it. When he had read it through twice, he looked at Lyons and said, "This is quite good. But does it go far enough? I think we need something more than just threats?"

"I agree," said Lyons, "that's why I thought sending them a piece of the stone might drive home the point."

"Yes," reflected O'Leary, "perhaps you are right. Have you anything else to report?"

"I believe that the King has asked Mr. Sherlock Holmes to look into this matter," said Lyons. "Kathleen told me that he paid a visit to her while she was working at Madame Tussaud's. Rather than risk exposure, she left the next day and is now living with her family in Clonakilty."

"That's too bad," mused O'Leary, "She has proven herself invaluable, but we have other eyes and ears in London."

After a pause, O'Leary said, "If you have the piece of stone with you, give it to me. I will have it packaged and posted from Dublin by one of the brothers. As for Mr. Holmes, I've heard of him. People say he's quite clever. Tell your boys and I'll tell the other captains to be on the lookout for any unfamiliar faces. My guess is that if he is trying to find the stone, he will come to Ireland. I'm hoping his English accent will betray him, but all the same, tell everyone to be vigilant and to be wary of any strangers."

Lyons said, "Tell the boys in Donegal to be especially alert. That's where Kathleen said she was from."

O'Leary laughed and said, "You have a good crew there Denis. Mr. Holmes may be clever, but together, I'll wager we are smarter. And if he causes any trouble for us, perhaps it's him that will find the bottom of a bog instead of the stone."

At that they all laughed, but had anyone caught the glint in O'Leary's eye, he would have known that his words were anything but idle threats.

Chapter 19 – Cork, Feb. 11-14

Sitting before the fire was a man with his back to me. I thought it might be Holmes, but having been fooled by my friend so often in the past, I refrained from saying anything.

Finally, he turned and looked directly at me. Were it not for the distinctive profile, I should never have known it was Holmes. His face was covered with soot. His tousled hair seemed matted and dirty, and he hadn't shaved since we had parted. He was dressed like a vagrant in the most disreputable clothes I have ever seen. The trousers were patched and dirty, the shirt might have been white at some point in the distant past, and the coat was torn and frayed in several places.

He looked at me for a long time as if gauging the effect of his appearance upon me and then he smiled and said, "It is so good to see you, Watson."

"You look far worse than when we left London, Holmes, if that's possible."

Holmes laughed, "I have been plying my trade, and I can assure you that it is not the neatest of professions. In the past three days, I must have cleaned at least 20 chimneys. Thus the state of my attire."

"Have you learned anything?" I asked.

"Yes," he replied, "before you start to clean a chimney, it is always best to learn how long since it was last swept.

Otherwise, you proceed at your own risk – a fact that I learned much to my chagrin."

"Holmes, you are impossible," I said.

"Oh, you meant, have I learned anything about the stone! Actually, I've had some small degree of success. It's amazing the things that people will say in front of someone they regard as insignificant. And more important are the things they utter when they simply forget that you are around, whether it be in the next room or up on the roof.

"I now know that there is a very strong chapter of the Irish Republican Brotherhood in Clonakilty, some 30 miles south of here. It's a small village, probably fewer than 1,000 people. It's located right near the tidal Clonakilty Bay, and the village is surrounded by hilly country, much of which is used by the local dairy farmers.

"While one stranger making his way into such a place would surely be noticed," Holmes said, "two would have the eyes of the entire town upon them."

"In this whole country," I asked, "what on Earth makes you think the stone is in such an out-of-the-way hamlet?"

"Because Mrs. O'Brien kept complaining to both Mrs. Sherwood and Mrs. Costello how her husband had to travel to Clonakilty every time the Brotherhood needed him. More important for our purposes, however, is the fact that Mr.

O'Brien is a carpenter by trade, and you will recall that I surmised that one of the men who helped steal the stone is a carpenter. By the way, he's quite a good craftsman, I must say."

"How did you learn all that?" I asked.

"I began by inquiring about carpenters in Cork. Mrs. O'Brien was the fifth carpenter's wife I visited. As luck would have it, I arrived at the O'Brien house late in the afternoon. As I had with my other customers, I offered to clean her chimney and promised that if she were not completely satisfied with my work, she would not have to pay me.

"While I was cleaning the flu in the living room, Mrs. O'Brien was in the kitchen with Mrs. Sherwood. I distinctly heard her mention the Brotherhood, which was followed by a litany of complaints. As I worked, I listened and I made certain that I was unable to finish that day.

"I told her how desperately dirty her chimneys were and showed her the handle of my borer, which I had deliberately broken myself.

"I'll get a new handle first thing in the morning," I said, "and then I'll come back and finish the bedroom and kitchen.

"She told me to leave the handle with her. She said her husband was a carpenter, and he could fashion me a new one without any trouble.

"When I returned the next morning, a new handle was waiting for me. After I did the bedroom fireplace, I was working in the kitchen when Mrs. Costello came to call.

"As they sat in the living room, I couldn't help but overhear their conversation. And you know what was even more interesting than the fact that her husband is a carpenter? He was in England recently, helping a friend transport his dead sister home.

"I have been an idiot, Watson! They didn't put it in a trunk, they hid it in a coffin."

"My word!" I exclaimed.

"Oh Watson, these are some devious rascals that we are dealing with."

"I'm beginning to appreciate that Holmes," I said, "So what will you do next?"

"I'm to Clonakilty," he replied, "plying my trade along the way. The more homes I service, the more my reputation spreads, and the safer I become because I'm not so much a stranger anymore, having cleaned Mrs. So-and-So's chimney. You see how it works?"

"And what am I to do?" I asked.

"You are to go to Shannonvale, a tiny village about four miles from Clonakilty and rent a small cottage if you can. I shall try to do the same thing near Darrara, another nearby town. I hope to make one of the cottages our base of operations, and we can meet there in the evenings, if circumstances permit – but only after I am certain that neither of us has been followed.

"During the day, you can look for work if you like. Try to keep to yourself, and if anyone should ask, you can tell them that your people came from Ireland, and after living and working in London, having been brought there as a child, you tired of England and decided to return home and spend your days in the land of your birth.

"Also, I instructed Mycroft to send any information that might come his way to the Ashe Street Post Office in Clonakilty to the attention of George Ward. So every other day, you must make the trek from Shannonvale to Clonakilty – although it's really not that far – to check for wires from Mycroft.

"But that need not happen for another few days. As I said, I must work my way to Clonakilty. In the meantime, you can stay in this cottage and enjoy the sights of Cork. Might I suggest a day at Blarney Castle where you can kiss the Blarney Stone?"

"Really, Holmes," I sniffed.

"I'm serious, Watson. There is one legend that holds that the Blarney Stone is actually a piece of the Stone of Scone, the very stone we seek."

"You aren't serious," I said.

"If you believe this particular story in lieu of the others, the Blarney Stone was presented to one Cormac McCarthy by Robert the Bruce in the early 14th century as a token of appreciation for McCarthy's support at the Battle of Bannockburn. It was then installed at McCarthy's castle of Blarney."

"I am astounded," I said.

"Don't be," said Holmes. "Other theories say that the Blarney Stone legend is only about 100 years old, and I know for a fact that the Blarney Stone is limestone while the Stone of Scone is a reddish sandstone. Remember Miss McMahon's replica and the rather distinctive colors? Still, people do love their legends, and you never know what you might learn."

"Holmes you are incorrigible," I said.

"So I've been told," he replied. "Now, in all seriousness, I have a big pot of Irish stew here that my last customer, Mrs. Donlevy, offered me as payment for my labors. I convinced her to throw in a loaf of bread, and I purchased a rather unimposing bottle of port. After all, looking as I do, I could hardly expect to be drinking anything better. Still, I tell you Watson, after a long day of sweeping, I find I've developed a ravenous appetite. I hope you are hungry as well, old man."

Although the fare was simple but hearty, the companionship made it seem like a feast. As Holmes and I chatted, I enjoyed myself tremendously, little suspecting how long it would be before he and I would enjoy a similar meal together.

Chapter 20 – Cork, Feb. 12-15

For the next three days, I puttered around Cork, remembering always to keeps my hands grimy. Although as a medical man, I cannot tell you how much it pained me to follow my friend's instructions.

I also remembered to change the lifts in my boot so that my limp would always be obvious.

I did make my way to Blarney Castle the first day. I rode on the Cork and Muskerry Light Railway, which travels 18 miles from Cork to Blarney. Primarily used by tourists, the local farmers and dairymen also employed it to transport their produce.

I attracted no attention, as I might have been either a poor tourist or a simple laborer. Upon arriving, I walked to the castle, where, after a long climb up a very narrow spiral staircase to the castle's battlements, I found two fellows who offered to sit on my legs so that I might lean out over the abyss and kiss this black rock known as the Blarney Stone.

Fortunately, I do not suffer from acrophobia, so I accepted their offer and gave them a few small coins when I had finished.

I felt no more eloquent after that exercise than I had before, and I now know more about the Blarney Stone than I care to admit. In retrospect, it seemed to me the perfect spot to commit murder and get away with it. After all, you merely had to sneeze and loosen your grip on the victim's legs and gravity would do the rest. I do believe that the fall would almost certainly prove fatal.

The second day as I was walking through Cork, a man asked if I were looking for work. I considered my appearance and decided someone of my station could ill afford to pass up the opportunity to earn some extra money, so I told him I was.

I spent the rest of the day unloading lorries that arrived at his dry-goods emporium. At the end of the day, I was given 50 pence and told that I could earn as much tomorrow if I returned.

With nothing else to do, I went back the next day and worked again. The owner, Mr. Thomas Crumblin, was so satisfied with my labor that he offered me a position, should I desire one. I made my apologies and told him that I had to go to Shannonvale to take care of some business, but I might consider his offer upon my return.

"Shannonvale, you say," said he, "I've people near there. If you need a place to stay, find the Crumblins, they have a dairy farm on the outskirts of Shannonvale, and tell them Tom sent you. No, better! I'll write you a note to give them."

I felt terrible about deceiving this good man, but I thought this might work to my advantage. Now, neither Holmes nor I would be total strangers in the village.

After he had finished, he put the paper in an envelope, sealed it and said, "You give this to me brother, Andrew, and he'll do right by you Mr. Ward."

I thanked him profusely and promised I would see him when I returned.

I slept well that night, and the next morning, I set out on foot for Shannonvale. I made my way along Dean Street to Gillabbey Street and then to College Road. A lorry driver, noticing my limp, asked where I was headed, when I told him, he said he would take me to Halfway and from there I could either walk – a distance of about 10 miles – or I might be lucky enough to find a farmer returning home.

We spent the morning talking about various subjects, and before I knew it, we had arrived at Halfway. I started on foot toward Shannonvale. Although it was January and the air was certainly crisp, it was a wonderfully clear day and the sun felt warm upon my face. I was comparing the beauty of the Gaelic countryside to the grubbiness of London, and wondering about the choices I had made in my life, when a voice interrupted my reverie.

"Where you headed stranger?" asked a man driving a wagon.

"Shannonvale," I answered. "I'm hoping to meet Andrew Crumblin. Do you know him?"

"I might," replied the man. "What's he look like?"

"I've never met him," I answered.

112

"Then why are you looking for him?"

"His brother, Thomas, told me to look him up."

"How do you know Tom?"

"I did some work for him," I answered.

"In the slaughterhouse?" he asked.

"No, in his dry-goods store. You ask an awful lot of questions," I said.

"We're suspicious of strangers in these parts," he said, "especially those with a British accent. But if Tommy Crumblin vouches for you, that's good enough for me. Climb aboard, I'll bring you to Andy's house."

After I had climbed up, he turned to me and extended his hand and said, "I'm Ray Carney, Andy's brother-in-law. I married his sister, Helen."

We talked about the weather and the countryside, and I kept waiting for the question to be asked.

Finally, I guess he could stand it no more, so Mr. Carney said, "I know you're meeting Andy Crumblin, but what brings you to such an out-of-the-way village as Shannonvale."

Since I had been expecting the question, I was ready with my answer. "My mother's family was originally from the area around Shannonvale and Darrara, and I'm hoping that I can find some of my people."

"And what would your mother's name be," he asked me.

"She was an O'Sullivan, before she married my father and moved to England with him."

"An O'Sullivan, you say. Lord knows we've a number of them in County Cork. I believe that there are several families in Darrara and nearby Clonakilty, and I am certain there's a passel of them in Shannonvale. Who knows Mr. Ward, you just may find that family after all."

He had stopped the wagon, and pointed toward a farmhouse in the distance. "That's the Crumblin place. Good luck, and I'm sure I'll be seeing you again."

I thanked him and waved to him as he drove off. Then I walked across the field and up to the front door. I knocked, and a man's voice from within said, "I don't know who you are or what you want, and I don't care. You can just head back across that field and be quick about it, or you'll be picking buckshot out of your backside for a week – if you live."

Chapter 21 – Clonakilty, Feb. 16

Although Kathleen Donnelly was glad to be home, she soon found herself longing to return to London. She missed the work at Madame Tussaud's, and she yearned for the return of her independence. She also wished that she could be free of Denis Lyons.

Perhaps there had been something there once. In retrospect, however, she supposed that it was nothing more than a deep friendship, reinforced by the common dream they shared of freedom for Ireland.

There were many things about Denis that she admired, including his intelligence, his passion and his eloquence. She knew, however, that her feelings would never match the ardor that he felt.

Her thoughts were interrupted by a sudden banging. Startled, she realized that Denis was hitting the desk with a book in an effort to call the meeting to order.

Looking around, she was struck by the fact that she was the only female in the room. She knew the other eight men. All of them were decent, hardworking individuals, and she realized that were it not for Denis's faith in her, there would have been a man sitting in her seat.

"Now that I have your attention," Lyons began, "there are a few things we need to go over."

"First, we are still waiting for the King and Mr. Gascoyne-Cecil to respond to our last communication."

"Surely, Gascoyne-Cecil will be on our side," said John Daly, an lawyer. "After all, he is responsible for the land reform, which has helped thousands of people here become property owners."

"I think that was done because he feared the alternative," said Lyons. "Let us not confuse political expediency with true friendship. No John, Mr. Gascoyne-Cecil may prove himself to be truly in our camp at some point, but I do not think he has done so yet."

"We shall see," was Daly's only rejoinder.

"In that same vein," continued Lyons, "we know that Mr. Sherlock Holmes has been brought in by the British government. We believe he has been commissioned to recover the stone.

"We know this because he visited Kathleen in her studio before she left London."

Suddenly, Kathleen felt all eyes, turning to look at her, and she heard Denis saying, "Kathleen, what can you tell us about Mr. Holmes?"

Standing, she said with a firm, clear voice, "I met him just the once. He pretended to be interested in papier-mâché, but his eyes darted everywhere, and he examined anything he could get his hands on quite carefully."

She continued, "He is quite tall and extremely thin. He has dark hair and piercing gray eyes. He is not an easy man to describe, but once you have met him, you will never forget him.

"I don't know how much help that is. The eyes are his most striking feature. They are quick and alert and they miss nothing."

"Thank you, Kathleen," said Lyons. "The good news here is that we think Kathleen may have sent Mr. Holmes to the north, but we cannot be certain. So I bring this to your attention because we must keep an eye out for strangers, especially those with an English accent."

"But people are constantly passing through," said Sean Dunhoy. "There are always peddlers, tradesmen and those preparing to leave Ireland for Scotland or America, coming from the west and heading for Cobh."

"I am not concerned about those passing through, Sean. I want you boys to keep your eyes skinned for those that linger – the worker that hangs around for more than a day or two. Do you understand?"

"I had a new chimney sweep at my house today," said Brian Barnewell, "and he's coming back tomorrow to finish the job. Do you want to come take a look at him?"

"Let us give this sweep another day or two. Then, if he's still here, we will consider paying him a visit."

The meeting then continued as the men discussed upcoming events and the recruitment of new members.

As they were about to leave, Lyons cleared his throat to attract their attention. "One last thing," he said, "and this is rather important. We all swore sacred oaths of secrecy when we joined the Brotherhood. Let us be mindful of that and be judicious with our speech – even around our families."

As the men were departing, Kathleen turned to go with them when she heard Lyons say, "Kathleen, a word?"

Fearing the worst, she turned to face Lyons, who then asked her very directly, "Do you think this Sherlock Holmes could disguise himself as a sweep or some other itinerant tradesman?"

Chapter 22 – Shannonvale, Feb. 16-17

Not knowing what to do, but deciding to take no chances, I said, "I'm leaving now, but before I do, I'm going to slip a note under the door."

After I had pushed the paper through the crack, I turned and started walking across the field back toward the road. I thought I head the door open, but I wasn't about to test his patience or my luck, so I refrained from turning around.

I had gone perhaps another 20 feet, when I heard a voice call out, "Mr. Ward! Mr. Ward! Please accept my apologies. As you might have guessed, I thought you were someone else entirely."

I wondered whom he might have been expecting that he felt it necessary to greet them with a shotgun, but I decided to let my host tell me his tale in his own good time.

"There's no harm done," I said. "It's just that I'm down this way looking for my people, and your brother – you are Andrew Crumblin?"

"Call me Andy," he interrupted me.

"Well, Andy," I said, "your brother Thomas suggested I look you up. I had been working for him, before I left Cork."

"Yes, yes, I see that," he said, "and Tommy says you're a right fine fellow. How can I help you Mr. Ward?"

"I'm hoping to rent a small cottage, while I see if I can find my family on my mother's side."

"And your mother's surname before she wed?"

"She was an O'Sullivan," I lied.

"Well, we've no shortage of O'Sullivans in these parts, and there's even more in Clonakilty. As for the cottage, I'd invite you to stay with me, but as you can see by looking at my home, there's nowhere to put you."

By now, we had reached the house, and he said, "Come in and have a cup of tea while I think where you might situate yourself."

"Do you live alone?" I asked.

"No," he said, "my wife and the children are visiting her sister over in Darrara. I expect them home shortly.

"You know," he continued, "there's a cousin of mine runs a boarding house in Shannonvale. It's not even three miles from here, and it's about the same to Clonakilty. I could write you a letter of introduction," he looked at me and laughed, "Don't worry, Mr. Ward. James doesn't even own a shotgun, so there's no danger there."

After he had prepared our tea, he set pen to paper and when he had finished, he folded it up, placed it in an envelope and said, "Give this to Jimmy Morton. He'll take good care of you."

He gave me directions and insisted that I take one of his horses, "Jimmy will get it back to me. Good luck Mr. Ward, and let me know how you progress in your search."

The horse moved at an easy trot and some 20 minutes later, I was standing in front of Morton's Boarding House on Old Cratloe Road in Shannonvale.

I knocked on the door, and a loud voice said, "Come in."

I entered and saw a tall, slender man, sitting in a chair, reading a book. He rose as I closed the door behind me. "My apologies," he said, "I thought it was my brother. Who might you be, and what can I do for you?"

I recited my story, gave him my note, and said, "Can you help me?"

"Certainly, Mr. Ward. I've a lovely room at the top of the stairs. Let me show it to you and see if it meets with your approval."

"You don't know of any cottages I can rent? I am a terrible snorer."

"Not at the moment," he replied. "Why don't you stay here for a day or two, and we'll see if we can't find you a place of your own."

I agreed and soon we were ascending a flight of stairs, so that he could show me the room.

"How much is it?" I asked.

"Normally, I get 10 pence a night, but seeing as how you come so highly recommended. I'll make it 8 pence a night, and if you pay a week in advance, it's yours for 50 pence."

"I'll take it," I said, handing him 50 pence.

"Wonderful," he exclaimed, "My only rule is no drinking in the house."

"That's fine," I said.

"I should also tell you that I have another lodger in that room." He pointed toward a closed door. "So, you'll have to share the bath."

"What about your family?" I asked.

"We sleep out back in a separate house. This is a building I inherited, and I use it to entertain and to bring in a little extra."

Reaching in his pocket, he produced two keys. "Here is the key to the front door and the key to your room. I'll lock the front now, I don't imagine my brother is coming this late.

"So, I'll see you in the morning, Mr. Ward. If you're interested, you can breakfast with us for an additional tuppence."

"Done," I said. Reaching into my pocket, I counted out 14 more pence and handed them to him.

"You are a gentleman, sir," he said, "And tomorrow, I'll point you in the direction of the O'Sullivans in Shannonvale, Darrara and Clonakilty."

"Thank you, Mr. Morton, and good night."

I entered my room, thinking things couldn't have gone better. I suddenly realized how tired I was. My head hit the pillow and I was soon fast asleep.

However, I woke shortly after and then sleep eluded me for quite some time as I wondered where Holmes might be and how he might be faring.

The next morning I dined with the Mortons and received a list of all the O'Sullivans they knew in Shannonvale, Darrara and Clonakilty. Since as you might expect there were more of them in the latter, it being the largest city, I told Mr. Morton, I would begin my searches there.

He told me that Eileen O'Sullivan lived on Wolfe Tone Street, and I would pass her house on my way into Clonakilty.

About 40 minutes later, I knocked on Eileen O'Sullivan's front door, and over a second cup of tea told her my tale. She did not have a sister named Bridget – the name I had given my fictitious mother – but she seemed to think there might have been a Bridget in the O'Sullivan clan that lived on Old Chapel Lane.

About an hour later, I found myself sitting with Rita O'Sullivan, who had a cousin named Bridget, but she had married an Ulsterman, she told me.

It was midday, and I decided to check at the Post Office for a wire from Mycroft. I found a telegram waiting for George Ward. Upon opening it, I saw the words. "Order received. Stop. Unable to fulfill it. Stop. Machine broken. Stop. Regrets, Banks."

I had no idea what any of it meant, but I put it in my pocket to keep it safe for Holmes.

I decided that I was hungry and opted to try my luck at Scannell's Public House.

The place was virtually empty and I found myself sitting alone. I ordered bangers and mash and a pint of Guinness, and was wondering how I might meet up with Holmes, when a boy walked over to me and asked, "Are you Mr. George Ward?"

I told him I was, and he said, "Mr. O'Sullivan asked me to give you this." He handed me an envelope, and I handed him a shilling.

I wondered which of the many O'Sullivans in that area was looking for me. I had met several women but had yet to encounter a male O'Sullivan. After he had left, I opened the note and read, "Start home to Shannonvale at 4 p.m. and I will find you on Old Timoleague Road."

My heart was racing. The note could have come only from Holmes, and I was excited at the prospect of seeing him again.

After my meal, I visited three more families of O'Sullivans in an effort to dispel suspicion and maintain my new-found identity. Looking at my watch, I saw that it was a few minutes before four, so I set out for Shannonvale on the route I had been told to follow.

About a mile outside of town, I saw a man struggling with a wagon. I wanted to be alone to meet Holmes, but my human nature got the better of me, so I said, "Do you need any assistance?"

Without turning around, he said in a thick brogue, "If you could just hold this axle for a minute, I'd be most grateful."

As I held the axle with both hands, he stepped back, looked at the wheel and then turned to me and said, "How were those sausages? They looked delicious."

Chapter 23 – Clonakilty, Feb. 17

"I don't know what's to be done," said Lyons. He was sitting with the men who had helped him steal the stone. The only one missing was Michael Collins, who had not been asked to attend.

"I think we have a stalemate," said Santry. "They won't give us our freedom, and we will most definitely not return the stone. However, I do see a glimmer of hope."

"And what might that be?" asked O'Brien.

"There has been no news about the coronation," replied Santry. "Surely, that bodes well for us. If they had the stone, I should think they would be announcing a date for King Edward to assume the throne. Without the stone, they find themselves waiting just as we are. And we have everything to gain."

"And everything to lose," interjected Lyons.

"How's that?" asked O'Brien.

Lyons replied, "We have done all that we can do. From now on, we must be passive. At the same time, the British have hired Sherlock Holmes and possibly other agents in an effort to recover the stone."

"We know that it's well-hidden," said Nesbitt, "and that's a fact. The only way they can possibly find the stone is if one of us talks."

"And that won't happen," said Santry. "We swore an oath when we joined the Brotherhood. Let us right now reaffirm that pledge that we will never betray our cause or reveal the hiding place of the stone."

They all agreed and pledged their sacred honor to the cause and the secret.

"And that is why I stressed that we must be ever vigilant," said Lyons. "Are there any strangers in town besides the sweep that Barnewell mentioned?"

"Yes," said Santry. "There's a fellow calls himself George Ward. He says he's here looking for his people. He claims his mother was an O'Sullivan."

"Do you believe his story?" asked Lyons.

"Well, I know he visited four O'Sullivan families today, so for the moment, I would say that he appears to be what he says he is."

"And how about the sweep? What do we make of him?" asked Lyons.

"He cleaned my neighbor's chimney," said Nesbitt, "and they were quite satisfied with the work. I was thinking of hiring him myself."

"Why don't you do that," said Lyons. "Be discreet, but see what you can find out about him. I don't like it when there's one outsider in Clonakilty, and the notion of two truly vexes me."

"We'll watch them," said Santry, "but they may be exactly what they say they are. After all Denis, there was a time when you were a newcomer to our village."

"True enough," said Lyons, "but I didn't show up in the weeks after one of the greatest robberies in the history of England – a robbery about which no one is talking – at least not publicly."

"Well, we know what to do with such men," said O'Brien. "Now, I've got to get on my way. I've a nice ride back to Cork and the comfort of my bed."

"Best to the family," said Lyons.

"I'll be on my way as well," said Nesbitt.

When they had left, Lyons looked at Santry and said, "They did good work in London, and they can talk of knowing what to do with such men, but I wonder if they would have the stomach for it, if it had to be done."

"I think Nesbitt would," said Santry, "O'Brien – I have my doubts. But it doesn't matter. If there's a bit of hard work to be done, you know you can count on me."

"And you on me," said Lyons. "Now, I'm going to see if I can find that sweep. It's not that I don't trust Nesbitt, but

I think I should like to meet this fellow face to face. If I send for you, you'll come immediately?"

"Of course," said Santry.

"Now, let us figure out what we can do to trip this man up on the chance that he isn't what he claims to be."

They discussed the possibilities for close to 30 minutes, and when they had finished, they were both quite pleased with the scheme that they had devised.

"As the great playwright once said, 'The play's the thing. Wherein I'll catch the conscience of the king.' I like this plan, Santry. I think it will bear fruit if we but nurture it carefully."

Chapter 24 – Shannonvale, Feb. 17

While I was excited to see Holmes, I also knew that it was imperative that we maintain our disguises. Holmes indicated as much by cautiously raising his finger to his lips.

After fixing the wagon, we continued walking toward both Shannonvale and Darrara. When we reached Ring Road, Holmes turned right and I followed. After about a half mile, he bade me wait in front of what appeared to be a deserted cottage while he ventured back down the road whence we had come.

After about 20 minutes, he returned and said in his broad brogue, "Hurry inside, and I'll see what I can do for you."

Once we had entered, he stretched and then he turned to me and said, "It is so good to see you, old friend. I notice that your limp is as obvious as ever. Well done, Watson! And how goes your quest for your long-lost mother? Fruitless, I hope."

As he spoke, he lit a fire and put on water for tea. "I'm afraid it won't be like Mrs. Hudson's, but it's the best I can do under the circumstances."

I could see that he was flushed with excitement, and I wondered if he would ever pause and allow me to speak.

Finally, I said, "Holmes, I've something for you."

He finally paused, "Oh, what might that be?"

I handed him the telegram, which he read several times.

Finally, I said, "It makes no sense to me."

"It's code, Watson. So if it had made sense, I should be extremely worried."

"Code?" I asked.

"Just a little something that Mycroft and I worked on before I left. Not at all like the one that you and I devised. The wire reads: 'Order received. Stop. Unable to fulfill it. Stop. Machine broken. Stop. Regrets Banks.'

"The phrase 'Order received' means another demand has been made. 'Unable to fulfill it' tells me that the crown will not comply. It's the last two phrases that are puzzling. Mycroft has sent me a message, but concealed it in the broadest possible terms."

I could see him turning the words over and over in his mind, searching for a combination that made sense.

As we sipped our tea, I knew there would no rest on his part until he had sorted it out.

After about 30 minutes of absolute silence and two pipes, he exclaimed, "I have been a blind beetle, Watson. 'Machine broken' is so obvious that I missed it looking for something far more subtle. It simply means that the demand was typed rather than handwritten and that something in the typewriter is amiss or 'broken.' The last word Banks, which can also be a synonym for shoals, tells me that the demand was composed on a Sholes and Glidden Type-Writer. I can only conclude that the word 'Regrets' is intended to point us to the letter 'R' on that particular machine."

"Bravo, Holmes," I exclaimed.

"Not at all, Watson. As you know I have devoted more than a little time to the study of typewriters and their individual characteristics. I might have finished my monograph several years ago, but new machines are constantly being introduced. Chief among them is the Remington No. 2, which allows typists to shift from lowercase letters to upper and back. Can you believe it? Researching it and all the other new developments has required a considerable amount of time on my part, and I still haven't completed my analysis. At any rate, I should like my work to be as comprehensive as possible."

And then he caught himself and started to laugh, "But I digress. We have some catching up to do, and I am certain that you are as interested in my progress as I am in yours.

"But first, however, I think we must eat. I am famished. I believe that I have told you that this sweeping does give a man an appetite."

He opened his bag and produced cured ham, cheese, a loaf of brown bread and a bottle of ale. "It isn't much," he said, "but if one were to look at us, it certainly befits men of our station."

I laughed, and said, "Indeed, it does. Now Holmes, tell me what you have been up to?"

As he set about preparing our simple meal, Holmes began recounting his adventures.

"I worked my way down here as I said I would, and my reputation did indeed precede me. There's not a housewife living that can refuse a bargain and the chance of getting her chimney cleaned for free. As a result, I have been working constantly. More important, I have been listening and observing. I think I can say with absolute certainty that the men who took the stone are all from Clonakilty – with O'Brien, the carpenter from Cork, being the obvious exception.

"I can also tell you that this small village is a hotbed of republicanism with its own chapter of the Irish Republican Brotherhood. So we must be on our guard because I am equally certain that they are expecting British agents."

"How can you be sure of that?"

"Because the men of the village have been meeting more frequently than usual in the past few days, and they have been instructed not to discuss the nature of their meetings with anyone – not even their wives – a fact that has Mrs. Nesbitt more than a little put out with her husband. By the way, would you believe that Mr. Nesbitt invited me for a nip after I had finished my work and then spent 20 minutes inquiring about my past and my family."

"What did you tell him?" I asked.

"That I never knew my father. That I was born in the Dublin Magdalen Asylum in Lower Leeson Street and raised by my mother in the workhouse at Portumna. I said that she had died when I was 10, and then I ran away. I told him that I learned my craft from an old man who had befriended me, and I have been living on the streets ever since. He can investigate all he likes Watson. The record-keeping at such places is notoriously poor."

I am always amazed at the detail which Holmes brings to bear on such situations.

"Nesbitt seemed to believe my story," Holmes continued. "Now, we must wait and see how it fares with his cohorts.

"By the way, Watson, you should know that you have attracted your fair share of attention, so you must keep up your inquiries for the foreseeable future. I have no doubt that if you can occupy their attention for just a day or two more, I may be able to make some serious inroads."

"I shall do my best," I promised.

"And now let us talk of other things while we eat," he said. "I am afraid that when we are finished, I have some grave matters to discuss with you."

Chapter 25 – Killarney, Feb. 18

Lyons stepped down from the train in Killarney. The new Clonakilty junction of the Cork, Bandon and South Coast Railway had made the journey much faster. Although the only heat in the cars was provided by foot-warmers, it was just an hour's journey from Clonakilty to Bantry where he then followed the Prince of Wales Route to Killarney.

"The world is changing," thought Lyons, "and we must certainly change with it."

Although he was fairly certain that he had not been followed, he wouldn't know with absolute certainty until a bit later. He strolled around the town, looking more like a tourist than a man on a mission.

Keeping careful track of the time, he let an hour pass, and then he purchased some flowers from a street vendor and headed for the cemetery. The road was deserted, and the wind was gusting. He was glad that he had worn an extra sweater.

Turning into the churchyard, he found the grave he sought and placed the flowers near the headstone. He crossed himself and said a few prayers.

From where he was standing, he could see the marker that he and his men had placed over the Coronation Stone. It looked undisturbed, and the thought filled him with relief. As long as the four of them kept their mouths closed, there was no way that anyone could ever find out where the Stone of Destiny had been concealed.

As he made his way back to the train station, he wondered what King Edward would do. As far as Lyons could tell, the King had but three options. He could be crowned without the stone – and break with centuries of tradition. He could try to pass the imitation stone that they had left in Westminster off as the original – a plan fraught with peril, for they would alert the press on both sides of the Irish Sea if the monarch should ever attempt such a maneuver.

The best of all the options would be for the King to grant Ireland its freedom.

And then a fourth possibility occurred to him. Just as they had done, the King could create his own Stone of Destiny, be crowned on it and scotch all their plans.

I can only hope His Majesty is not that devious, thought Lyons, but then he paused. "If I thought of that option, certainly someone else will suggest it to the King. How can we forestall the possibility?" he wondered.

He continued mulling over the problem all the way to the train station. As he waited, he studied a map of the tracks, and he realized there was no way the monarchy could attempt to create a new stone. The iron rings, centuries old, could not be duplicated. Certainly, they could acquire ancient rings from some other monument, but any cuts made to a stone, to insert the rings would be easily detected by even an amateur geologist. The same applied to any effort to mimic the cross that had been crudely inscribed on one side of the stone. The cuts would give them away. All they would have to do would be to alert the press that a fraud of royal proportions was being perpetrated on the citizens of Great Britain.

No, he decided, a second stone was not really a viable option for the Crown.

So once again, we arrive at an impasse. We will simply bide our time. King Edward will bide his, and eventually, he must assume the throne without the stone or free Ireland.

As he boarded the train, he took a seat at one end of the car. Except for two women, who were traveling with an infant, he had the entire carriage to himself. He was rather enjoying the scenery when his reveries were interrupted as Santry lowered himself into the seat across from him.

"And must we do this three times a week?" asked Santry.

"It's a precaution," said Lyons. "There are two strangers in our village that we know of, and perhaps others of whom we are ignorant. Any or all of them might be there on behalf of King Edward.

"Should any of them take the train and follow me to Killarney, we will have our man."

"But why lead them to the churchyard?" asked Santry.

"I am known in Killarney. My parents are buried there, and my presence there, especially as a dutiful son come to pray for his parents, will arouse no suspicion."

"I think it's an unnecessary risk," said Santry.

"We are taking a chance, I grant you that. However, if it helps to preserve our secret, then I think it is a gamble that we must take."

"And if we see a stranger following you from Clonakilty to Killarney?" asked Santry.

"Well then, we can only hope that whoever it is didn't waste his money on a round-trip ticket," said Lyons, without the least bit of irony in his voice.

Chapter 26 – Shannonvale, Feb. 17-18

When we had finished, we both began to smoke. After a bit, I said, "Holmes, I believe you said you had some serious matters to discuss with me."

"No," said Holmes smiling, "I believe the word I used was 'grave'."

"So it was," I said. "What of it?"

"I meant 'grave' in quite a literal sense, Watson. We know that whoever took the stone smuggled it out of England in a coffin. What better way to hide the stone than by burying it in that same coffin?"

"Brilliant Holmes. There is only one problem," I said.

"Yes, yes, I know," he replied, "Ireland is filled with churchyards and cemeteries. There must be hundreds of graveyards and thousands upon thousands of grave markers. However, it falls to us to locate the needle in the haystack. After all, even if we were to confront the men who took the stone, I rather doubt they would oblige us with its location."

"So what's to be done?" I asked.

"Well, you have ready access to the local graveyards in your search for the elusive Bridget O'Sullivan. Be on the lookout for any newly dug graves. Should you spot one, try in your own circumspect manner to make certain that the individual buried there is the same person whose name appears on the tombstone – if there is one.

"I don't expect you will have much luck. I think these men are smart enough to bury it far away from their own town, which only leaves us a large portion of the rest of the country to worry about."

"If you think I am on a fool's errand, then why don't I pursue another line of inquiry?"

"This is one case, where we really must leave no stone unturned," chuckled Holmes.

In spite of myself, I found myself laughing at my friend's *bon mot*.

"Well done Holmes," I exclaimed.

After we had discussed a few more items, Holmes said, "Now, you must head back to your rooming house. I shall meet you in the same place in three days' time, and if you should see me on the street?"

"I know. I'm to ignore you. What will you be doing?" I asked.

"Sweeping and listening," said Holmes, and "praying that neither of us wears out our welcome.

"However, I do need you to send a wire to Mycroft for me. You will send it to Mr. James O'Connell in Dublin – he is one of Mycroft's agents there. He will forward it to Mycroft and when he receives a reply, he will send a wire to Mr. Ward at the Ashe Street Post Office."

"What is it you need to know?" I asked.

"Here is the cable," said Holmes, and he handed me a piece of paper.

I read it over, but since it was in code, I could not make total sense of it; however, I did find several words rather suggestive. At any rate, for those readers enamored of puzzles, here is the text:

"How many machines? Stop. It is a serious concern. Stop. Are we missing any pieces? Stop. Eagerly awaiting reply. Stop"

I returned to the Morton household, and after sending the cable the next day, I proceeded about my business. Since I had called upon half of the O'Sullivans in Clonakilty, I was growing fearful that I might exhaust all of the possibilities before we had made any significant progress.

At one point the following day, I did see Holmes from a distance, pushing a cart filled with the tools of his trade and looking like the world's grimiest sweep. I rather doubt that he saw me, although if he had, he didn't give even the slightest indication.

I was headed back to my room late that afternoon when I spotted another familiar face on the other side of Clogheen Road. There was no mistaking that lustrous red hair and that dazzling smile. Coming out of a dressmaker's shop was the woman whom Holmes and I had visited at Madame Tussaud's in London. She had called herself Kathleen McMahon, but I now believed that to be her *nom de guerre*.

I was trying to figure out how I might learn her real name when the shopkeeper threw open the door and shouted after her, "Kathleen!"

The woman turned and the shopkeeper held up a bag, saying, "Don't forget this bonnet. You promised you'd have it ready for me tomorrow."

I thought, "So Kathleen is her real Christian name, but what might her surname be?"

I couldn't hear what she said to the woman, but I determined to follow her. Staying far back, I watched her walk out of town and then she turned onto O'Rahilly Street. After about five minutes, she entered the front yard of a well-kept cottage. As she opened the door, I could hear her say, "I'm home."

I thought this is real progress. So I waited for another ten minutes and finally a young boy came along. "Excuse me, my lad. Is that the O'Sullivan house?" I said pointing at the cottage.

"No sir," he replied, "the Donnellys live there."

"Are there any O'Sullivans around here?" I asked.

He stopped and thought, and finally he said, "The only ones I know live on Casement Street." And he proceeded to give me directions. I gave the lad a copper for his troubles, and felt that I had accomplished a great deal.

As I made my way back to Shannonvale, I couldn't decide whether I was more excited about my discovery or the prospect of seeing Holmes the next afternoon.

I also wondered how much longer we would have to carry on this charade. I longed to shave regularly, and wash my hands thoroughly and pull that irritating lift out of my boot. And I wanted my moustache back. Sometimes Holmes' suggestions work a little too well.

The next day seemed to last forever. I checked at the Ashe Street station around noon and found a cable waiting for me. I knew there was no point in reading it, since it would make sense only to Holmes, so I stuffed it in my pocket.

Finally, I found myself on Old Timoleague Road at four o'clock. Every time someone would approach, I would slip into the woods until eventually, in the distance, I saw Holmes pulling his cart.

I knew that he had spotted me, so I quickened my pace and headed directly for his cottage so that we might not be seen together.

I slipped inside and a few minutes later, Holmes entered.

"I have news for you," I exclaimed.

"Yes. I am certain that you do," said Holmes. "Pray tell me what you've learned."

I then proceeded to tell him about Kathleen Donnelly.

"You have done well, Watson. And did you know that whispers have her romantically linked to the schoolmaster, Denis Lyons?"

"How could you possibly know that?" I asked.

"Because I cleaned her mother's chimney yesterday. Mrs. Donnelly is a charming woman in her own way, and she does enjoy her gossip. In fact, I would describe as a veritable font of information."

I can only suppose that Holmes must have seen my crestfallen expression before I turned away. He put his hand on my shoulder and said, "Now, now, don't be dispirited, Watson. I certainly had no intention of stealing your thunder – only to enhance it with a little lightning."

His tone was so sincere, I could not remain angry. "And have you made any other progress?" I asked.

"Indeed," he said, "I believe that now I know the culprit, but the location of the stone eludes me still."

"You know who took the stone?"

"I believe I do, but in this case the who is not nearly so important as the where."

He continued, "Since we first began this case, I have been asking myself incessantly: What would I do were I in their shoes? I can now trace their movements with uncanny accuracy up to a point, and then I lose the scent entirely."

"What's to be done?" I asked.

"We continue to persevere," said Holmes.

"Oh, I had almost forgotten. I received a cable today." I handed him the wire, and he proceeded to read it over.

When he had finished, he looked at me and said, "This is another step in the right direction. Now, how did you make out with your graveyard inspections?"

"Just as you predicted I would. There have been five burials in the past two weeks, and from talking with the various O'Sullivans, they either knew all the victims or were related to them in some way.

"I visited the cemetery and counted five new graves and no more," I added.

"Excellent," said Holmes.

"Now let us take stock of our progress thus far," he continued. "We know that Queen Victoria was buried February 4. I believe that we can safely assume the stone was stolen early on the morning of the burial. If everything worked in their favor, they could have had it here the next night or at worst, the following morning.

"Since the trip to England lasted but five days and they were back with their families two days after the funeral, they must have buried the stone within a day's ride of Clonakilty.

"You see, Watson, we are narrowing the hunt, little by little. We cannot see our quarry, but we know it is there.

"What gives me pause," said Holmes, "is the possibility that our quarry is expecting us.

"Now, here is what you must do, old friend," he said, and he then proceeded to outline a very detailed course of action for me.

When he had finished, I said, "Are you certain this is how you wish to proceed?"

"No, Watson. I am not certain at all, but at the moment, I can see no other way. Just remember one thing, while we are trying to run them to ground, they are doing everything possible to elude us – and if I am reading them correctly, they are also setting traps of their own."

"So be on your guard, Watson. I am counting on you," said Holmes.

At that moment, I vowed that I would not fail my friend, no matter what perils might present themselves to me.

Chapter 27 – Killarney and Clonakilty, Feb. 19-20

Denis Lyons made his second trip to the cemetery in Killarney without incident. He and Santry agreed that no one had followed him.

As they made their way home, Lyons said, "Is that sweep still in Clonakilty?"

"I believe he is," replied Santry.

"I should very much like to meet with him, and then we will address the matter of Mr. Ward, who claims to be a distant relative of one of the O'Sullivans, if he is still among us. Odd, that his mother never told him more about her family, don't you think."

"Not so much," replied Santry. "There's plenty of women here who would like nothing more than to escape their fathers and brothers – and some with good reason. Consider how many gave up their children and how many others ended up in the workhouses."

"You always did have a tender heart," said Lyons.

"It's not that," said Santry, "I'm just trying to keep things in perspective. Sometimes you become so consumed with the cause that you lose sight of other things that might be equally important."

"Nothing is as important as our freedom," said Lyons.

"Not to you certainly. But I'm willing to bet there are plenty of others who don't share our point of view. Sometimes, you seem almost overzealous in your passion. It can be a bit frightening."

They sat in silence for quite the better part of an hour, and when the train pulled into the Clonakilty Junction station, Lyons clapped Santry on the back and said, "We must remain united, my friend. Now, I'm off to get my chimney cleaned."

As Lyons walked home, he knew that he had to find a way to press the issue. Then it hit him. The British government had entrusted Sherlock Holmes with finding the stone, if we can frustrate their efforts either by capturing Holmes – or killing him if it should come to that – the King and Prime Minister might not remain so obdurate.

They would get their stone back and the highly regarded Holmes, if he were still alive, and Ireland would be free.

Now, all he had to do was make certain that neither the sweep nor the ubiquitous Mr. Ward was Holmes in disguise. And then he could set about focusing on other possible targets.

Of the two, he thought Ward the more likely candidate. After all, he had an English accent and he was basically inviting himself into people's homes – and perhaps their confidence – with his sad tale of seeking out his people.

The sweep by all accounts had proven to be excellent at his trade, and from what Nesbitt had been able to glean, he seemed to have a lived a hard life. Plus, Lyons was having difficulty convincing himself that a gentleman such as Holmes would know how to do an honest day's work. "Consulting detective, indeed!" he scoffed.

As he mulled it over and over in his mind, he suddenly knew exactly how he would bait his trap.

"You may be the toast of London, Mr. Holmes," he thought, "but I'm guessing that if we should encounter one another, you will find yourself wishing that you had remained there. The last thing you want to do is run afoul of the Brotherhood, and by accepting the King's commission, you have done exactly that."

Before heading home, Lyons knew that he had one more call to pay, and it was a visit that he was eagerly anticipating. With his mind made up now that he could see everything clearly, he set out for O'Rahilly Street.

After 20 minutes, Lyons had arrived at the Donnelly home. He was welcomed inside and was delighted to learn that Kathleen was at home.

When she came into the room, he was, as always, stunned by her beauty. Composing himself as best he could, he said, "We need to talk. It's just twilight out. Would you care to go for a stroll?"

She could tell by his demeanor and the tone in his voice that it was something important. So she said, "I'll get my coat."

As they walked along, Lyons told her everything he had been thinking about Holmes.

"If you were to meet Holmes again, and he were disguised, do you think you might recognize him?"

Thinking it over, she replied, "Perhaps. As I said at the meeting, his eyes are quite distinctive. I don't think I shall ever forget them."

"That's what I am counting on," said Lyons.

After he had finished, she said, "The sweep cleaned my mother's chimney the other day, and she was quite pleased with him."

"Did you see him?"

"No," she replied. "I was at the dress shop."

"I must admit that does give me pause," he said. "I wonder if Holmes would know how to clean a chimney, let alone do a good job of it."

He then proceeded to outline his plan, telling her everything, including the fact that he was favoring Ward as Holmes rather than the sweep.

When he had finished, she exclaimed, "Denis, that is absolutely brilliant! I should not like to be Mr. Sherlock Holmes and have to match wits with you."

"It's only brilliant, if it works," he said.

"I shall do my part. You may count on me."

"I know that," he replied. "So, then, I shall set things in motion tomorrow."

The next morning he awoke, ate breakfast and set out to find the sweep.

After several inquiries, Lyons learned that the sweep was busy cleaning Mrs. Gallagher's chimney. Within ten minutes, he had arrived at the house. When Mrs. Gallagher answered his knock, he said, "I understand we have a new sweep passing through."

"That's right," she beamed. "He's up on the roof right now."

"Pray tell, what is he doing up there?"

"You may ask him yourself," said Mrs. Gallagher. "Here he is coming down now."

Lyons looked to his right and saw a man descending a ladder.

"I'm almost done on the roof," said the man with a broad Northern brogue.

"No trace of an English accent there," Lyons said to himself.

Taking him in, Lyons saw that he was six feet tall, perhaps a bit less, and he was bundled up against the cold, so it was hard to say whether he were tending toward stout or, in fact, quite lean. He also noticed that the man's eyes were a dark brown and exceedingly red and bloodshot, as though they were quite irritated. Lyons didn't find that unusual, given the soot that must be in his face all day.

His hands were absolutely filthy and his clothes, worn and patched in various places, had all seen far better days.

"Can you do another chimney today?" asked Lyons. "I'm afraid I've been rather remiss in that area."

"I could certainly use the work, Mr....," the man's voice trailed off.

"Lyons," he replied. "I'm the schoolmaster here in Clonakilty, and I am not terribly handy around the house. You are?"

"My Christian name is Paul, but I answer to 'sweep' as well."

"How long will it take you to finish here, Paul?"

"Oh, another few hours, sir. I have two more fireplaces to tend to, and then I must do my clean-up work."

"How exactly do you clean a chimney?" asked Lyons innocently.

"The first thing I do is close the damper. Then I cover the fireplace opening and the floor around it. Then up to the roof and clean the cap if there be one and brush the chimney flue from the top with my brushes and my borer if the soot be very heavy.

"Then after I've made certain that the flue is as clean as I can get it, I lower a lantern down the chimney on a string trying to make certain that everything is as it should be. Then I come back in and clean the firebox and smoke shelf, which is what I'm going to do now in the kitchen. Finally, I check to make sure the damper is working all right and that it is safe to use.

"Then I tidy up any mess that I may have made, and if there be more than one chimney in the house, like this one, I do it all again," he laughed.

"So how long before you're finished here?" pressed Lyons.

"Another few hours or so, and then I've promised to do the O'Grady chimneys. Can I come to your house tomorrow?"

"That would be splendid," said Lyons. "Do not trouble yourself about lunch. I will provide it."

"That's very kind of you sir. Where do you live?"

Lyons gave him the address and directions and said, "I have a few errands to run in the morning. Why don't we arrange to meet at my house at one o'clock?"

"Whatever you say, sir," said Paul and then he added, "I'd shake your hand, but," holding up his thoroughly blackened hands, he said, "I hope you will understand."

"Certainly," said Lyons, "I shall expect you around one."

As he left, Lyons thought, "He certainly appears honest enough, but we will know for certain by tomorrow afternoon whether this sweep is really what he seems."

Chapter 28 – Cork and Clonakilty, Feb. 19-20

The next day, I traveled to Cork, walking some of the way and riding with farmers for sections. After arriving in Cork, I then continued on to Midleton, where I sent several cables on Holmes' behalf. I instructed all those receiving them to address their replies to Sgt. George Ward, care of the main post office in Midleton.

Holmes had explained that he was fearful of using the post office in Clonakilty any longer, and he was equally loath to have me use the one in Cork, where I was known by a few people. Although you could have counted them on a single hand, in Holmes' opinion that was still too many.

I must admit that while I understood the nature of one or two of his inquiries, there were several that baffled me. However, I did as my friend had requested and soldiered on.

I found lodgings for the evening in a modest boardinghouse, and the next morning when I returned to the post office, I discovered that all of the previous day's communiqués had been answered.

After hiding all of the wires in a special pocket in my bag, I set out for Cork and then Clonakilty. It was early evening by the time I had reached Shannonvale. Mrs. Morten was kind enough to prepare a meal for me, and as I ate, I chatted with her husband.

"So, have you had any luck with your people," he asked solicitously.

"No," I said with a tinge of regret. "I've a few more families to try, but I'm beginning to lose hope. However, I shall persevere," I assured him. "I haven't come this far to leave the job unfinished."

After I had eaten my meal, I bade my host goodnight. As I was about to leave, he said, "Mr. Ward, a word."

"Yes," I said.

He looked almost embarrassed, but finally he said, "Will you be staying another week? I have a possible tenant for your room next week."

Since I had no idea how long we would be required to stay in the area, I paid him in advance for another week and said, "You must let me know immediately if that should happen again. I do like the room, and as I said, I am determined to finish my quest."

The next morning, I made my way to Clonakilty, where I called upon two more O'Sullivan families and then treated myself to lunch in the public house. While I was eating, I noticed a young lad standing outside without a hat or gloves and doing absolutely nothing.

Knowing Holmes' penchant for using youngsters to follow people, I wondered if this boy had been assigned to me. I decided to pay another visit to the local cemetery. There was plenty of open ground, which would make it very difficult for him to hide.

Although he stayed with me for a few moments, when I arrived at the cemetery, I was alone. Determined to be on my guard, I headed back through town, intending to meet Holmes near his cottage.

It was by pure chance that I spied the boy trying to conceal himself in an alley as I walked by. I pretended to take no notice, but I thought to myself, "Our quarry may not know we are here, but they most certainly suspect that someone is coming their way."

I considered confronting the youngster but then thought better of it. So I decided to try another way, I was heading for the church when I saw a young woman of about 20 grab the boy and say, "Michael, Ma has been looking everywhere for you."

I desperately wanted to hear his answer, but he turned from me and said something to her in a voice so low that it was inaudible. However, I was glad to see her prevail and despite the boy's protestations, she took hold of his sleeve and started dragging him in the opposite direction.

I made my way to the church, entered and knelt in prayer. When no one else came in, I left by a different door. After making certain that I had no unwelcome companions, I headed for the Old Timoleague Road and the safety of Holmes' cottage.

He wasn't there when I arrived, so I let myself in and sat down to wait for him.

It was some 20 minutes later that Holmes opened the door and said, "What have you for me, Watson?"

I handed him the wires which he opened and perused one by one.

Before reading the last one, he looked at me and said, "We are definitely making progress, my friend, but this next communiqué is crucial. If I do not receive some assistance, by way of an answer from Mycroft, I shall have to devise an entirely new plan of attack."

With that he ripped open the envelope, read the cable three or four times. Unable to bear the suspense any longer, I broke the silence with the word, "Well?"

"It is not what I was expecting, Watson. I suppose that would have been too much to hope for, but I believe there is enough here to allow us to continue on our present course."

"Well surely then, if we can continue, you must be on the right track," I said.

"That is certainly true," said Holmes. "Now, it is a question of tactics.

"Let us consider," he said, talking more to himself than to me, "We know who took the stone. We know where it is – in the most general terms. All that remains is for us is to pinpoint its exact location, and after today, I think I have an idea on how we may do that."

"Besides the wires, did anything else happen today?"

"Oh, Watson. I do apologize. Today has been a day of revelations. Let us prepare something to eat and, over dinner, I shall tell you about my encounter with one Kathleen Donnelly, she of the lustrous auburn hair and the decidedly fetching smile."

"You met her?" I asked incredulously.

"I shall tell you all about it as soon as we have fried these fish that I just purchased," he said.

Knowing that to press him would be futile, I asked, "What can I do to help?"

"You may peel the potatoes," he replied. "The story I am about to tell you is, I think, best savored over a hearty meal."

After we had finished all the preparation work, Holmes said, "Let me start my story while we are waiting." He took one chair by the fire while I took the other. After lighting his pipe, he turned to me, and now that I could see his face, I was stunned.

"Holmes!" I exclaimed. "Your eyes are brown! How on earth?"

"I was wondering when you'd notice," Holmes said. "Actually, they've been brown since I arrived in Ireland."

"But how? You have always had gray eyes. And now they are quite brown!"

"Yes, you have made a point of describing the color of my eyes in several of your narratives. I thought that being able to change their color might one day prove invaluable, and I was right.

"As you know Leonardo da Vinci had suggested several centuries ago that the optics of the eye could be altered by placing the cornea directly in contact with water. However, it wasn't until 1827 that the astronomer Sir John Herschel suggested that making a mold of one's eyes might enable the production of lenses that would conform to the surface of the eye. And then it was another 60 years or so later that the German glassblower F.A. Muller employed Herschel's ideas to create what he called 'a special glass lens.' His work was duplicated shortly after by the Swiss physician Adolf E. Fick, and the Paris optician Edouard Kalt.

"On one of my trips to the Continent, I visited Monsieur Kalt, and he made two pairs of lenses for me. They do not correct my vision, which, as you know, is quite good, but they do change the color of my eyes.

"And that bit of foresight may well have saved my life today. Now, let me remove these as they do tend to irritate the eyes after several hours, and then I shall bring you up to date on my endeavors."

Holmes then proceeded to remove an extremely thin glass lens from each eye.

He placed them on a white cloth so that I might examine them. They were so fragile that I was almost afraid to touch them. After I had looked at them, he placed them in a hard case.

"And you say these saved your life?"

"Indeed, they did," Holmes said.

161

He paused before announcing, "It was a trap, Watson!"

Chapter 29 – Shannonvale, Feb. 21

"Yes, Watson. It was a very carefully planned gambit, but a trap nonetheless!"

"What on Earth happened?"

"While cleaning Mrs. Gallagher's chimney, I was approached by Mr. Lyons, who hired me to sweep his chimney. My suspicions were aroused immediately, so I was on my guard.

"We arranged to meet the next afternoon. As soon as I entered his home, I detected just the faintest hint of lavender in the air. No doubt you remember that when we met Miss Kathleen McMahon at Madame Tussaud's, she too was wearing a rather distinctive fragrance with a hint of lavender.

"At any rate, I set about sweeping his chimney. After I had finished on the roof, I began to clean the fireplace. I was kneeling on the floor when I heard Lyons say, 'Mr. Holmes?'

"Since I was expecting something of the sort, I ignored him totally. He tried it a second time, and I refused to react, continuing about my business.

"Finally, I felt on a hand on my shoulder, and I turned and found myself looking at Kathleen Donnelly. My respect for her grows daily, Watson.

"She said, 'Mr. Holmes, would you care for some lunch?'

"I said, 'I'm sorry m'lady. My name is Paul, Paul Grogan. I think you've mistaken me for someone else.'

"She stared intently at my eyes, Watson. I know she was looking for the gray that you have oft described. And that is why I say; those little pieces of glass saved my life.

"She apologized, of course, and said I reminded her of a sweep that she had encountered at her aunt's a year or so ago.

"I should think he must have been quite a fellow," I said, "and we all laughed. However, I could tell she was still uneasy. She rather reminds me of *the woman*."

"Now Holmes," I said.

He continued as though he hadn't heard me. "After I had finished, Lyons gave me two pounds."

"I said, 'That's far too much, sir. Do you have another chimney I can clean? Perhaps at the school?'"

"Lyons thought that was a capital idea, so I'm to meet him at the school tomorrow."

"Why are you cleaning the school chimney?" I asked.

"Because from what I could gather, there is no typewriter of any sort in Lyons' home. I am hopeful of finding one at the school, and should it be a Sholes and Glidden Type-Writer with a defective 'R,' well then, we will have our suspicions confirmed and know with absolute certainty that Lyons is indeed involved in the theft of the stone."

"Well, that is progress," I remarked.

"Yes, and I found one other thing that has piqued my interest," said Holmes.

"It seems as though Mr. Lyons has been to Killarney twice this week. I don't know what it means, but I do find it curious that he went there twice in three days."

"That is rather odd," I said. "How did you discover that?"

"He was kind enough to leave the tickets on the nightstand in his bedroom?"

"It could be another trap," I ventured.

"Indeed, it could," said Holmes. "Things may get a bit dicey from here on out. They are obviously looking for us. That much is evident from Miss Donnelly's presence at Lyons' home and her offer of lunch. If I have successfully fooled them, I cannot help but think that they will brace you next, Watson, so best to be on your guard."

"Well, if they are looking for your gray eyes, they certainly won't find them on me," I laughed.

I then proceeded to tell Holmes about the boy that I thought was following me.

"I'm sure you are right, Watson, so you must be very careful."

"Now, what about those wires you received?" I asked.

"One was from Mycroft, informing me that 24 Sholes and Glidden Type-Writers have been shipped to Cork in the last five years. As near as he can tell, only two have made their way to Clonakilty. Whether they remain here or whether others have arrived via a more circuitous route, he cannot say with any degree of certainty."

"And the others?"

"I had asked Mycroft to look into any reports of missing tombstones."

"Why would you do that?"

"Because if you are going to smuggle the stone out of England in a coffin, as I believe they have done, the next logical step is to bury the coffin and then camouflage it with a grave marker."

"And what did Mycroft discover?"

"Oddly enough, there have been several reports of stolen tombstones. None near here, unfortunately."

"That would have been too easy," I observed.

"Yes," remarked Holmes. "All of the missing markers, four to be exact, occurred in various counties far to the north. Two went missing from Londonderry, one from Armagh and one from Donegal. Given the distance, I can only ascribe those thefts to the strained relations between Catholics and Protestants in that part of the country. Otherwise, they make no sense."

"There are times when I think this entire case makes no sense," I sniffed.

"I shouldn't let the King hear that," Holmes countered.

As we laughed for what seemed the first time in weeks, Holmes announced that the potatoes had cooked, and we would be eating in three minutes.

Had I known what we would encounter in the not-too-distant future, I think I might have eaten that humble fare with a much greater appreciation for ordinary creature comforts.

Chapter 30 – Clonakilty, Feb. 21-22

"Well, now that you have seen him, what do you think?" asked Lyons.

"There are certain qualities about him that make me think he might be Holmes," answered Kathleen.

She continued, "His height is about the same, but given all the clothes he was wearing, I found it difficult to estimate his weight."

"Yes," said Lyons, "but I saw no reaction on his part when I called for Mr. Holmes, did you?"

"No."

"And you insisted that Holmes' eyes were gray and his most distinctive feature, and to me the man's eyes were quite clearly brown, were they not?"

"Yes," she replied, "they were definitely brown. I don't see how you can counterfeit that."

"I trust your intuition, Kathleen, but I think in this instance, you may be so overwrought that your mind is playing tricks on you."

"I'm sure you are right," she said, but inwardly she vowed to keep a close watch on Paul, the chimney sweep extraordinaire.

"Now, I shall turn my attention to Sgt. Ward, who has been too long in the area for my taste, but first I'm going to take advantage of the sweep's offer and have him clean the chimney at the school."

"Why would you do that?" she asked.

"Because the chimney needs cleaning, and I think one more meeting will afford me an additional opportunity to see whether this fellow might be Holmes in disguise, although I rather doubt that it is."

"Shall I walk you home, Kathleen?" asked Lyons.

"That won't be necessary. Besides, I have a few errands to run before dinner."

"Fine," said Lyons. "Be well, and I shall call upon you shortly and let you know how things turn out, both with the sweep and Sgt. Ward."

As she walked along the street, Kathleen replayed the encounter with the sweep over and over in her mind. There was something slightly off that had happened, but she couldn't quite put her finger on it.

"Perhaps if I leave it alone for a bit and look at it with fresh eyes tomorrow, it will come to me," she thought.

But try as she might not to think of it, there was something nagging at the back of her mind.

* * *

The next day Lyons met the sweep at the schoolhouse.

As he showed him the building, he explained, "It's a central chimney that draws from four fireplaces. Do you have to clean all of them?"

"Don't you want me to?" asked the sweep.

"Of course, just be very careful in the headmaster's office," Lyons said, pointing to one of the doors, "and whatever you do, don't touch anything. He's a stickler, and a firm believer in a place for everything and everything in its place."

"I understand, sir," said the sweep.

"I'll be back in an hour," said Lyons.

"I'll start with the headmaster's office," said the sweep. "That way you can inspect it when you return."

"Very good," said Lyons, and off he strode.

After setting a ladder against the roof, the sweep entered the headmaster's office and secured a heavy cloth in front of the fireplace. Going to the window, he could make out Lyons striding down the road in the distance. Looking about he was disappointed to discover that there was no typewriter in sight.

Before continuing the search, he checked the other rooms just to be certain, and then he hung up cloths in front of each fireplace.

Returning to the headmaster's office, he went to the roll-top desk in the corner. "This looks promising," he thought. Although it was locked, he produced a leather case from his pocket and from it extracted a slender pick.

The lock was no challenge and as Holmes rolled up the cover, he found a relatively new Sholes and Glidden Type-Writer sitting there. Inserting a piece of paper into the cylindrical platen, he then hit all the keys twice. He couldn't see what he was typing because the keys were hidden inside the machine.

After he had gone through the alphabet a third time, he removed the paper.

"This may warrant a special section in my monograph," thought Holmes, who immediately folded the paper up and concealed it in his shoe.

He then locked the desk and proceeded to sweep the chimney and clean up the mess his efforts had produced in each of the four fireplaces.

He was just about finished in the larger of the two classrooms, when he heard a voice call out, "Paul, where have you gotten to?"

"I'm not sure what he's up to," thought Holmes, "but I can only suspect that it is some kind of trap."

Steeling himself, Holmes called out, "I'm in the classroom, Mr. Lyons. I'm on the last fireplace. Almost done."

"Well, when you've finished, step into the headmaster's office, I've something that I would like very much to show you."

"I'll be along presently, sir. Just let me tidy up here."

"Don't dally."

"As you wish, sir."

Not knowing what to expect, Holmes walked to the headmaster's door and knocked.

"Come in, Paul. There's no need to stand on formality. You're among friends," said Lyons.

As he entered, Holmes knew immediately that something was terribly amiss.

"I'm going to ask you some questions," said Lyons, "and I want you to think very carefully before you answer them. Do you understand?"

"Yes sir," said Holmes, trying to sound intimidated.

"Did you touch anything in this office?"

"I'm afraid that I did, sir," said Holmes. "I was curious, 'cause I never went to school, so I was looking at everything."

"Are you a thief, Paul?"

"Sir?"

"Did you break into that roll-top desk?"

Knowing he had been caught in the act, Holmes decided that the truth might be his best defense. "I did, sir."

"How did you do it? And, more important, why did you do it?"

"I'm afraid me curiosity got the better of me, sir. I picked the lock and examined that fancy writing machine."

Taking stock of his surroundings, Holmes focused on a tall cupboard in the corner. "Surely, there was someone concealed in there," he thought, berating himself for not searching the room more carefully. And as he examined it further, he concluded that only a very slight adult or a child could fit in such a small place.

"Did you type anything?" asked Lyons.

"Just some letters. I can't really read," he said.

"Where is the paper?" asked Lyons.

"I put it in me shoe. The sole is wearing thin in one spot and I thought it might provide a bit of padding."

"Let me see it," said Lyons.

"Taking off his shoe, Holmes extracted the paper and tried to hand it to Lyons.

Looking at it rather distastefully, Lyons said, "Just unfold it, please, and show it to me."

After he had examined the keystrokes and saw that they made no sense, Lyons said, "You are a good worker, but I find now that I can neither trust you, nor can I recommend you. Let me suggest that you pack your things and ply your trade in another village. Do I make myself clear?"

"Yes sir," said Holmes, "and thank you sir. I am truly sorry for what I've done." He then folded the paper up again and tucked it back into his shoe.

"If I may though, sir, just one question?"

"What is it?" asked Lyons.

"How did you catch me, sir?

Lyons laughed and said "Michael, come out and say goodbye to Paul."

With that, a young lad, about nine or ten, stepped out of the locker.

"Oh, very good, sir. Very clever."

"Now," said Lyons, "it is time for you to go, and if I ever see you in these parts again, I'll make you wish I hadn't."

"Yes, sir. Thank you, sir. I'll just gather me things and be on me way."

As he exited the headmaster's office, Holmes left the door slightly ajar. It wasn't much, but it allowed him to hear Lyons say to the boy, "Now Michael, go tell Mr. Santry to come to my house at five, and we can figure out how we are going to deal with Sgt. Ward."

Chapter 31 – Clonakilty, Feb. 22

I spent the day visiting with the last two O'Sullivan families in Clonakilty. Given that fact, I wasn't quite certain how much longer I was going to be able to maintain the charade.

I was just about to head to the public house when I was knocked to the ground by the cart Holmes was pulling.

He reached down to pull me up and as he brushed me off, he said, loudly enough for anyone in the immediate vicinity to hear, "I'm so dreadfully sorry, sir. It's my fault entirely for not looking where I was going. Are you hurt, sir?"

"No," I said sternly, "but you really need to be more careful."

"I will, sir. I promise."

And with that he trudged out of town on the Old Timoleague Road, looking for all the world like a beaten dog.

I knew the encounter had been intentional, but Holmes had said nothing of substance. Discreetly, I began to check my pockets. In my coat, I could feel a small piece of paper that I knew had not been there earlier in the day.

Knowing better than to take it out in public, I proceeded to the public house. In the water closet, I examined the note, which said, "Leave now."

Not knowing what was amiss, I lit a cigarette and then with the match burned the paper.

I had no idea why Holmes had gotten the wind up, but I knew better than to doubt my friend.

After quickly finishing my pint, I set out on Boyle Street and then doubled back on myself by taking Convent Way and walking the circle that was Convent Court. After I was absolutely certain that I was not being followed, I made my way to Old Timoleague Road and headed for the cottage, stopping occasionally to smoke a cigarette – and to make certain that no one was trailing behind me.

When I finally arrived at the cottage, I knocked and was instructed to enter.

I found that Holmes had shed his disguise and was looking a great deal like his old self, gray eyes and all.

He was standing by the fire, examining a sheet of paper with his lens.

"So good to see you, Watson. I trust you took precautions to make certain that no one followed you."

"I did indeed."

"Splendid," he said. After taking a brief glance out the window, he continued, "What do you make of these letters?"

He then handed me a page on which the entire alphabet had been typed three times.

After looking at the words for several seconds, I asked, "What does this mean?"

Holmes said, "When I was cleaning the school chimneys, I discovered a Sholes and Glidden Type-Writer in the headmaster's office. I really needed to see only the 'R' but I decided to hide it amidst the other letters just in case something unexpected should occur."

"And?"

"I was careless, Watson, and I almost paid dearly for my oversight. Lyons had concealed a young lad in a cupboard who told him everything I had done."

"How did you manage to escape?"

"By admitting my transgressions, cowering a bit, and promising to leave Clonakilty at once. As I was packing up, I was fortunate enough to overhear that they next intended to deal with Sgt. Ward.

"Deciding there was little else to be learned in the village, I deemed it best that we both make a speedy departure.

Now, if you would like to shed your disguise, I've soap, a razor and some clean clothes waiting for you."

"But Holmes," I interjected.

"There will be plenty of time for conversation and explanations later. Right now, I suggest we make our way to Cork by a fairly circuitous route, and once we are underway, I will be more than happy to answer all of your questions."

After I had shaved and washed, taken the lift out of my shoe and changed my clothes, Holmes and I set out for Cork, using the back roads.

As we walked, Holmes would occasionally cast a surreptitious glance over his shoulder.

"We are not being followed, are we?" I asked. "I took several precautions."

"I am sure you did, old friend, but there are many of them, and only one of you. Besides, I was the one who was followed."

"You?" I exclaimed. "You mean you knew you were being followed?"

"I'm afraid I do," said Holmes.

"But aren't you concerned? Needn't we be worried?"

"Not at all," said Holmes. "Actually, now that I know he is the only one tailing us, everything is falling into place quite nicely."

"Who is following us?" I asked.

"The same boy who was hiding in the schoolroom closet. I don't think he will be with us much longer. Oh, how I would like to hear his report to Mr. Lyons," Holmes said.

Abruptly changing the subject, he looked at me and said, "I am certain that had we the note here that Mycroft received, we would have indisputable proof that Lyons is our man."

He continued, "I know you didn't have much time to examine the letters I typed, but the 'R' has a slight bend to it. You can see that the stem of the letter is hitting the paper much more forcefully than the tail – as though it had been bent or mispositioned ever so slightly."

"So what do we do now?"

"We watch Mr. Lyons very carefully," replied Holmes. "He is obviously traveling to Killarney for a reason. If I had to guess, I'd say that he is trying to bait anyone who might be suspicious of him into following him. My guess is that he has a confederate on the train, watching for just such a thing."

"Holmes, there must be a hundred cemeteries in and around Killarney. With no idea what to look for, how will we ever find the right one?"

"Well, to begin with, the cemetery where the stone is hidden cannot be too far from the station. If Lyons can make it from Clonakilty to Killarney and back in several hours, then he must not have too far to travel once he arrives in the city. I should think that would limit our searches to perhaps ten or 20 graveyards rather than a hundred."

"Yes," I replied, "You have certainly eliminated any number of choices, but that still leaves us with the task of hoping that we have chosen the right cemeteries. And if we have, there are still hundreds of acres to be covered and thousands of tombstones to be examined."

"I certainly cannot fault your logic, Watson, but I think we may further refine our search."

"How so?"

Holmes then proceeded to elucidate all the factors that he believed had played into Lyons' decision in selecting a hiding place for the stone. "I realize that I am theorizing without all the necessary facts, and as you know such is anathema to me. However, in this case, I find myself forced to violate my own rules," he admitted.

After some reflection, Holmes remarked. "I'll say it again, Mr. Lyons has proven to be a worthy foe indeed. I should almost hate to hand him over to the authorities."

"You can't be serious," I exclaimed.

"He has harmed no one. He has taken something, which may rightfully belong in this country anyway, and he has yet to show himself a blackguard. No, Watson, I'm rather enjoying the challenge he has presented, and I think you know me well enough to understand that I will always do the right thing – or at least make an effort in that direction."

After a rather considerable trek, we found ourselves passing a meadow where a farmer was tending his cows.

"Have you a cart?" asked Holmes.

"Yes, sir" replied the farmer.

"Would you like to earn a guinea?"

"Indeed, I would sir."

"Then get your cart and drive us to Cork. I will make it worth your while," said Holmes.

Ten minutes later, we were sitting in the back of the cart, headed for Cork. I wasn't quite certain where we were bound after that, but I knew that Holmes had a plan, and he would put it into motion as soon as we arrived at our destination.

Several hours later, we reached the outskirts of Cork. Holmes then gave the fellow two guineas and made him promise to say that he had never seen us.

"Will he keep his word?" I asked.

"I think he will, Watson. He seemed an honest chap, struggling to get by. Besides, he knows that we can find him again, should we so desire.

"Now, let us purchase some new clothes, enjoy a fine dinner, cooked by someone else for a change, and sleep in a real bed. I'm done with this hardscrabble life for the foreseeable future," he said.

"However, I must admit that I do see some tramping about in our near future, so make certain that you purchase comfortable boots."

"I had almost forgotten about that," I said.

"I'm rather inclined to think that things won't be as bad as you anticipate. Tomorrow, after I have contacted Mycroft and received answers to several questions, I think we will know a great deal more about the direction our paths will take."

It was odd to see Holmes so optimistic, and I found myself wondering whether he had learned something that he had yet to share with me.

Chapter 32 – Clonakilty, Feb. 22

"Go on Michael. Don't be afraid. Tell Mr. Lyons what you saw," said Kathleen.

"After I left you, I ran to Mr. Santry and delivered your message. And as I was walking along, I saw the chimney sweep knock another man down in the street with his cart," said the boy.

"That's no crime," said Lyons, "he was probably still on edge from the tongue-lashing I gave him."

"I rather doubt that your threats scared Mr. Sherlock Holmes," said Kathleen bitterly.

"What are you saying?" asked Lyons.

"Let the boy finish," said Kathleen.

"After the sweep helped the other man up, I continued following him," said Michael.

"Why were you following him?" asked Lyons.

"Miss Kathleen had told me to," said the youngster.

"Will you let the boy finish," said Kathleen.

"Go on," said Lyons.

"I followed the sweep to a cottage on Ring Road, out off Old Timoleague Road. I was hiding in the woods, watching the place, when all of a sudden the man who got knocked down comes limping along. He knocked on the door and went inside. I wanted to get closer and see what they were doing, but I was afraid they might catch me."

"That was very smart," said Lyons.

"After a while, the door opens and two proper gentlemen come out, and they start walking north toward Ballinascarty."

He continued, "As soon as I thought it was safe, I ran to the cottage, There was no one inside. So the sweep and the other man…"

"Must have been in disguise," said Lyons, finishing the sentence for him.

"Describe the men you saw walking away," said Kathleen.

"One was very tall and very thin," said Michael, "and the other was shorter, a bit stouter and looked like a soldier. I followed them for a while and then I came right back here."

"Holmes and Watson," said Kathleen.

"How could I have been so stupid?" asked Lyons. "We had them here, and we let them slip right through our clutches."

"You can go now, Michael," said Kathleen.

"Thank you ma'am."

Lyons handed the boy a shilling.

"You needn't do that, sir," said Michael.

"No, but you have earned it," said Lyons, "Once again, you have done good work, and such labor should always be rewarded. Now, go along and buy yourself something you will enjoy."

"If it's all the same to you, sir, I'd rather give it to me Ma," said the lad.

"It's your money, Michael, now off with you."

After the boy had left, Lyons looked at Kathleen and said, "Why did you have the lad following the sweep?"

"There was something wrong about my meeting with him. It kept nagging at me. Finally, I decided that it was the fact that he didn't react in any way when you called to him. He didn't turn his head, even slightly. It was as though he forced himself not to react.

"I know the eyes were the wrong color, and he certainly looked nothing at all like the Holmes I had seen in London. Perhaps now that we know he is also a master of disguise, we can turn that to our advantage at some point."

"I hope you are right," Lyons said. "But I must confess that I am a bit concerned about the stone. If Holmes could track us here, there is always the possibility that something we said or did provided him with a hint as to its hiding place."

"Do you think it is well hidden?" asked Kathleen.

"Yes, I believe that it is."

"Then leave it be. From now on, we must act as though we are being watched at all times. Even if there are no strangers in Clonakilty at present, not everyone here is sympathetic to our cause. With the right persuasion, Holmes may have convinced one or two of our neighbors to keep an eye on us."

"I'm not certain that I like the path we are treading, Kathleen."

"It would not be my choice either," she replied, "but I think it falls to us to make the best of a bad situation."

"I believe then it behooves us to send an ultimatum to King Edward. Either free Ireland or give up any hope of being crowned on the stone."

"Haven't we already done that?" she asked.

"We have, but this time we are going to give His Highness a very strict deadline. He can either meet it or suffer the consequences. If he makes even the slightest concession at all, we will have scored a victory of sorts."

"And if he does not?"

"Then we leave the stone where it is, and go on about our business as though none of this had ever happened. There are only four people who know exactly where the stone is hidden, and I'm certain that while they would like nothing more than to toast the liberation of Eire, they will not be crushed if we are forced to resume our old lives as though nothing had ever happened."

"I suppose you are right," she said. "I suspect that even if we are not given our freedom, we can still celebrate. After all, how many people can say that they humbled the British monarchy and outwitted the great Sherlock Holmes? All things considered, I think those are two accomplishments that you can be pretty proud of Denis."

"Thank you, Kathleen."

"Don't be thanking me just yet," she cautioned. "Holmes is still out there somewhere, and the sooner we know where he is and what he is up to, the happier I will be."

"And how do you propose, we do that?" he asked.

She then explained her plan to him, and when she had finished, he looked at her and said, "That is absolutely brilliant. I wonder if Mr. Holmes has any inkling of the storm that is headed his way."

"I do not know, nor do I care," she laughed.

"Now, let us set things in motion, for the sooner we get things started, the sooner we will see results. I shall cable the lads in Dublin, Wexford, Waterford, Cork and Killarney. Something tells me they have headed for a big city."

"I agree," she said, "but I don't think they have gone too far, so for now, tell the men in Cork, Waterford and Killarney to be especially sharp. And tell them just to watch and report back to you. We know how slippery and how dangerous Mr. Holmes can be, they do not."

"Oh Kathleen, to have another chance at that bounder. I am in your debt."

As he moved toward her, she grabbed her shawl and said, "I've got to be going. It's past eight and my Mum will be worried sick."

"I'll walk you home," he offered.

"You have better things to do," she reminded him, and then she was out the door. The only sign that she had been there was a faint scent of lavender lingering in the air.

"You beat me once, Mr. Holmes, but I can guarantee you that it will not happen a second time," said Lyons to himself.

Chapter 33 – Cork, Feb. 23

The next morning, Holmes knocked on the door of my room. "Come on, Watson! It is nearly ten. If you sleep any later, you are going to miss breakfast entirely."

"Just give me a few minutes, and I'll meet you in the dining room," I replied.

After a quick wash, I combed my hair and headed downstairs. I found Holmes sitting in a distant corner of the spacious dining room. He was as far from any other patron as possible. What struck me as even more unusual was the fact that he was sitting in shadow, right next to a window that afforded a beautiful view of the city on a lovely, sunny day.

"I've taken the liberty of ordering breakfast for you, Watson. Poached eggs, toast and tea?"

"Thank you, Holmes," I said. "You seem very chipper this morning. Have you received some good news?"

"I have, Watson. I think my inquiry to Mycroft may have reduced the number of graveyards that we must search."

"Splendid!" I replied.

"Yes, it seems that before Mr. Lyons moved to the village of Clonakilty, he was a resident of Killarney." He continued, "Now, Watson, if you wanted to hide a coffin, and you needed to check on it occasionally, where would you conceal it?"

I was mulling the question over in my mind when my breakfast arrived. After I had attacked the eggs and toast, I said, "I think I should put it in the most remote cemetery that I could find. One that is seldom visited. Perhaps, one that has been deserted, and then I should check on it only at night, so as not to be seen."

"Bravo, Watson. You have done just the opposite of everything that I should do."

"Really?"

"Truly. You see if you put it in a remote cemetery, the chances of your being seen going there, I think, are greatly increased. Anyone, anyone at all, who might spot you, would most certainly wonder why is that man here, and what is he doing. More important, perhaps though, is the fact that as a stranger you would be remembered because you would have drawn attention to yourself.

"As for visiting only at night, an unknown individual spotted in a cemetery might easily be arrested on suspicion of grave-robbing. No, Watson, I'm afraid that won't do at all."

"Well, what would you do?" I sniffed, "Hide it in plain sight?" Sometimes his condescension can be maddening.

"Not in plain sight, Watson. But I would conceal it so that I could see it whenever I wanted to. Now, I know that sounds a bit of a contradiction, but I am certain that if you give it some thought, you will certainly tumble to it."

"Sounds more like a bit of twaddle to me," I replied. "Conceal it so that I could see it whenever I wanted to," I said, repeating Holmes' phrase word for word. Try as I might, I could not grasp the concept of how something could be concealed and yet visible at the same time.

"I've got it," I exclaimed after a few minutes.

"Do tell," said Holmes.

"You said the Coronation Stone had a cross inscribed on it, did you not?" I asked, and Holmes nodded in assent. "They stood it up in a graveyard, just like any other tombstone. That way they could see it from a distance and all the while it stood there masquerading as a marker."

"Bravo, Watson. There is definitely something to be said for that line of thought. However, it has no name, no dates, no writing of any kind; moreover, it has those iron rings. No, Watson, I'm afraid, the Coronation Stone will never be mistaken for a grave marker. But you have opened up a line of inquiry about the nature of gravestones that I intend to pursue."

"Have I?"

"Indeed, you have pointed me in a direction I had not heretofore considered. Now, not to change the subject, but have you noticed those fellows loitering across the street in front of the tobacconist?" Holmes asked.

Looking out, I saw two men in their 30s, standing across the street. "Do you mean those two fellows reading newspapers?"

"Yes. They have been standing there since I came down to breakfast. Neither has moved, and neither seems particularly interested in his paper."

"Do you think they are looking for us?"

"I shouldn't be surprised if there were two such fellows keeping an eye on every hotel in Cork, and perhaps several other nearby cities."

He continued, "It's quite obvious that the Irish Republican Brotherhood now knows for certain that we are in Ireland. My guess is that having eluded them in Clonakilty, they do not know exactly where we are, so they have assigned lookouts to each hotel in hopes of discovering our location and then, having done that, keeping a close watch on our comings and goings."

"To what end?" I asked.

"Perhaps we are getting close to the stone, or perhaps they just want to know the whereabouts of their enemies at all times."

"So what are we do? We certainly cannot move freely if they are following us."

"I quite agree, so here is what I want you to do," said Holmes, who then proceeded to outline his plan to me.

And so it was that a few minutes later, I found myself approaching our watchers. "Good morning, gentlemen. I am Dr. John Watson, and I am here at the behest of Mr. Sherlock Holmes. You are?"

"I'm Dave," stammered the taller of the two, quite obviously taken aback by my forwardness.

"And I'm Jimmy," replied the other.

"At any rate, Mister Holmes has been watching you, watching the hotel, and he wonders if you might care to join us for breakfast."

To say that they were dumbstruck would not even begin to scratch the surface of their befuddlement.

They looked at each other, and their indecision was as obvious as their hunger.

"They serve wonderful poached eggs," I continued, "and Mr. Holmes would be delighted if you would be his guests."

"You mean he wants to buy us breakfast?" said the one who had called himself Dave.

"Indeed, he does," I replied.

"Whaddaya think Jimmy?" he said.

His companion replied, "Nobody said we couldn't eat if we found them, and nobody said we couldn't enjoy ourselves a bit."

"Should we report in first?" said Dave.

"You can send a cable from the hotel." I interjected, "and they will be clearing the dining room fairly soon to prepare for lunch."

I think the thought of a free meal and possibly a free cable proved too much.

"Lead on, Dr. Watson," said Jimmy.

So we walked across the street and entered the hotel. As we neared the dining room, I pointed to a solitary figure sitting in the far corner with his back to us and said, "That is Mr. Holmes."

Just as we were about to enter the dining room, the hotel manager approached and said, "Dr. Watson, a word please."

"Gentlemen, you go ahead. I shall join you presently."

As they entered the room, I turned and sprinted through the lobby and out a side entrance where I found Holmes waiting for me in a cab.

"Bravo, Watson. Now we can be on our way – without fear of interruption."

"Who was that in the corner?" I asked.

"The house detective," replied Holmes.

"And where are we headed?"

"Come Watson, where has this case been leading us ever since we arrived in the Emerald Isle?"

"I have no idea," I said.

"We are going to Killarney, the ancestral home of one Mr. Denis Lyons, and unless I miss my guess completely, the current resting place of the Coronation Stone."

Chapter 34 – Clonakilty, Feb. 26

For obvious reasons, it took two days for word of what had become known as the "Cork Catastrophe" to make its way back to Denis Lyons.

No one wanted to break the news, but finally James Santry agreed to do it. After he had explained what had happened, Lyons' reaction was rather predictable.

"Mother of God! You cannot be serious," thundered Lyons.

"I'm afraid I am," said Santry.

"Let me see if I follow you," said Lyons. "This Dr. Watson walks up to our watchers, introduces himself and then invites them to join Holmes and himself for breakfast? And after they accept, but before you can say 'gone,' they discover that they are actually dining with the hotel detective?"

"That's it in a nutshell," said Santry.

"Oh, we really must stiffen the requirements for membership in the Brotherhood. Numbers are one thing, but if you have an army of idiots, it doesn't much matter how many men you have."

Having seen Lyons angry before, Santry knew that arguing would be pointless, so he remained silent.

"Do we have any idea where Holmes and Watson are now?"

"No. They appear to have vanished."

"He is not a magician," said Lyons. "He cannot make himself disappear. I'm willing to bet that he is still in the country, and if he is, we must find him as quickly as possible. Tell the boys they have to be on their toes. One more slip-up like that and it could be our last."

"What are you going to do?" asked Santry.

"I'm going to do Holmes one better," said Lyons. And then he explained to Santry what he had planned, and how Santry could reach him if he were needed.

"Are you sure you don't want me to go with you?" asked Santry.

"No, James. I think this is one mission that is best carried out solo."

"I suppose you are right," said Santry. "Suppose I follow you and get off the stop before? That way I'm not too far, and if you should need help, I can be there in a fairly short time."

"Excellent!" said Lyons. "I believe that we shall have the best of Mr. Sherlock Holmes yet."

A short time later, Lyons walked to the telegraph office and sent several wires. Then he proceeded to the schoolhouse where he picked up a few items. After that he went to the station, bought a train ticket to Killarney and sat down to wait.

All alone, he began to play out the endgame in his head. "If Holmes should do this, we can counter with that." And on and on he ruminated, trying to envision as many possible scenarios as he could.

"It's combat," he thought, imagining himself sitting at a chessboard with Holmes on the other side. And then it hit him. In truth, he had absolutely no idea of what Sherlock Holmes really looked like. Telling the stationmaster that he had forgotten something and would catch the next train, he hurried to Kathleen's house.

Fortunately, she was home. After outlining his plan to her, he then explained his dilemma. "And that is why I need you to come to Killarney with me."

"Denis, can you not let it be? He doesn't know where the stone is, and I rather doubt he's going to go digging up graves on a hunch."

"Kathleen, he has bested us at every turn thus far. He came into our village. He entered into our houses – both yours and mine – under false pretenses. If Mr. Holmes were so disposed, and with just a little bit of luck on his part, he could be the reason that we spend the rest of our lives in that miserable Crumlin Road Prison. Can't you just see him standing in the witness box, giving testimony against us?

"No Kathleen," he continued, "We have come too far to turn back now. And we have risked too much and sacrificed too much to let a busybody like Holmes prove our undoing."

"I'll go with you on one condition," said Kathleen.

"What might that be?"

"There is to be no violence. You can have your set-to with Mr. Holmes, but you must be prepared to walk away. England has not acceded to your demands because King Edward doesn't feel that he must. If you should harm Holmes, I don't know how the British might react, but I can promise you this. They will send another and another and another – they may not be as clever as Holmes – but eventually they will find the stone, and then all this will truly have been for naught. But if you just walk away, they can look for the stone for years – perhaps they will find it, perhaps they won't. But they will have no reason to come looking for us.

"Do I make myself clear?" she finished.

"Yes. I don't like it, but I do see your point," Lyons admitted. "I give you my word that I will do no violence to either Mr. Holmes or Dr. Watson."

"Do you swear?"

"On the souls of my sainted parents," Lyons said.

"I'm going to hold you to that Denis. Please don't disappoint me."

All the while Lyons was thinking. "I will do no violence, but I can't speak for the rest of the boys."

Before she could raise any further objections, he told her to pack a bag and gave her very specific instructions with regard to what she should bring.

Thirty minutes later, they were back at the platform where Lyons purchased a second ticket for Kathleen. Also sitting on the platform waiting for the train was James Santry.

They exchanged pleasantries, and Santry said he was going to visit a sick relative in Kenmare. When the train arrived, Lyons and Kathleen sat in one car while Santry took a seat in another.

And so within the hour, they were on their way to Killarney where Lyons was determined to bring Sherlock Holmes to heel – or die trying if need be.

Chapter 35 – Killarney, Feb. 24-26

Holmes had decided that it were best if we approached Killarney cautiously. So we kept our carriage and told the driver to take us to Millstreet, which was about midway between Cork and Killarney. Although the driver grumbled, Holmes told him that he would make it worth his while.

Along the way, Holmes outlined his plan, using me as a sounding board. After he had finished, I said, "Well, it's all well and good, but if you are wrong…"

"I know, Watson. But I do think I have come to a greater understanding of Mr. Lyons, and having placed myself in his shoes, I think I know exactly how he would have proceeded."

"Have you heard from Mycroft?" I inquired.

"Yes. He has proven incredibly useful, and I am certain that he has accomplished everything without leaving the comfort of the Diogenes Club or the confines of his office."

We continued talking and when we arrived in Millstreet, decided to have an early dinner. As we ate, Holmes said to me, "I am quite certain that they will be looking for two men traveling together. I want you to proceed to the Railway Hotel in Killarney. I am going to try to find accommodations in Kilcummin, a small village about three miles from Killarney.

"The important thing to remember is that the only one who can identify us with certainty is Miss Donnelly. Lyons has only seen us in our disguises, so I rather think she will be accompanying him.

"After you check in, feel free to stroll about the town. I would try to avoid deserted streets. After all, should she spot you without you knowing it – just as you did her – you never know if they may assign someone to follow you. I can assure you that the thought of you as a prisoner in the hands of the Irish Republican Brotherhood would give me pause and might persuade me to drop the case altogether. However, if you should encounter Miss Donnelly, which I am inclined to think is a possibility, I am counting on you to keep her occupied."

While I was touched by my friend's rare show of emotion, I buckled up and responded simply, "That's an awful lot to ask, old man," I said. "And what will you be doing?"

"I shall be looking for the stone, of course. I have a number of inquiries I must make, and I am hoping that one of them will bear fruit," he replied. And he then proceeded to tell me in general terms exactly what he hoped to accomplish.

After dinner, I hailed a carriage, and told the driver I wished to go to the Railway Hotel in Killarney. As we drove down the street, I turned to wave once more to Holmes, but when I did, I saw that he had already vanished.

I didn't know how long it would be before I would see my friend again, but I couldn't escape the feeling that we were rushing headlong into a situation that was, to a large degree, totally beyond our control.

After checking into the Railway Hotel, I enjoyed a wonderful night's sleep, and the next morning I wandered down to the dining room. I was quite taken with a saying on the menu that advised: "Eat breakfast like a king, lunch like a prince and dinner like a pauper."

Deciding to take the advice to heart, I ordered smoked salmon and scrambled eggs. After several cups of tea and a generous helping of toast with fresh Irish butter, I set out to explore the cemeteries of Killarney – on a sort of busman's holiday.

My first stop was at the Aghadoe Cemetery, which I was told had acted as the main burial ground for Killarney and its environs for centuries. It was less than five miles away, and my carriage had me there in about 45 minutes.

Although I had only the vaguest notion of what I was looking for and absolutely no idea of what I might find, it seemed as good a choice as any.

Upon arriving at the graveyard, I was immediately struck by the differences in tombstone design between Ireland and England. There were all different types of Celtic crosses dotting the landscape. The workmanship on some of the stones was very intricate and quite beautiful.

However, many of the stones were so old and weathered that reading the inscriptions was next to impossible. I thought I might mention that to Holmes and see if he were willing to change his opinion about the Coronation Stone passing as a tombstone.

At one point, I spotted a groundskeeper and asked if there had been any recent burials. He informed me that the cemetery was always busy and that funerals occurred just about every other day.

Uncertain of exactly how to proceed, I finished strolling the grounds, enjoying the sun on an unseasonably warm day. I was quite taken with the intricate carvings on the stones as well as the various shapes of the crosses and I wondered what mysteries a trained eye might be able to unravel.

The view with the lakes and Ross Castle in the distance made it seem ideal for a holiday destination. After a few hours of aimless wandering, I returned to my hotel, but there was no word from Holmes.

The next day, I started out to see a section of Killarney National Park. Located south and west of the city, the park is a staggering expanse of rugged mountainous country. Among the many attractions are McGillycuddy's Reeks, the highest mountain range in Ireland. Located at the foot of the mountains are the world famous Lakes of Killarney.

The park offers a beautiful blend of mountains, lakes, woods and waterfalls, and the terrain seems to be ever-changing. As you might expect, there is a certain majesty to this unspoiled area. Throughout my excursions, I kept careful watch to see if I were being followed.

Among the other attractions in the park are Ross Castle, Innisfallen Island and Muckross House and Gardens. I was informed by the hotel concierge, an elderly gent with a vast reservoir of local knowledge, that the latter had been preserved as a late 19th-century mansion featuring all the requisite furnishings and artifacts of the period. He had stressed that it was not to be missed.

He had also told me that the land had been in the Herbert family for more than two centuries. However, in 1899, the family, beset by a series of financial problems, had been forced to end their stay at Muckross and had sold the land to Lord Ardilaun, a member of the Guinness family.

After a short carriage ride, I found myself standing in front of Muckross House. To say it is an imposing structure would not begin to do it justice.

The guidebook that I had purchased at the hotel informed me that the mansion had been designed by the architect William Burn for Henry Arthur Herbert and his wife Mary Balfour Herbert. Construction had begun in 1839 and the home was finished in 1843, shortly before the Great Famine.

An amateur watercolourist, Mrs. Herbert had achieved no small degree of renown for her work, and I vaguely recalled that several of her paintings had been presented to Queen Victoria as gifts.

In fact, if the concierge were to be believed, the Herberts had spent so much money refurbishing the estate for the Queen's visit in 1861 that they never quite recovered financially, and that brief royal stay was what would ultimately cost them the estate years later.

The guidebook also included the fact that Henry Herbert had requested that he be buried standing up as he thought the view of the Lakes of Killarney could not be matched by anything in heaven.

After a brief walk to the Killegy cemetery, which is about a half mile from Muckross House, my real reason for visiting the park, I asked a gravedigger where I might find Henry Herbert's tomb. He gave me directions and after a short trek, I found myself standing in front of an enormous Celtic cross that dominated that section of the cemetery.

While the tomb is not very long, it is definitely elevated enough for him to have had his final wish granted. At the base of the cross was a plaque erected by his tenants that testified to his sense of virtue and their grief at his loss. I thought it a most touching sentiment.

Outside of the spectacular panorama, I could discern little else in the graveyard that might prove of interest to either Holmes or myself.

After a stroll around the small cemetery, during which I kept looking for anything that seemed as though it might not belong, I headed north for Muckross Abbey, about a mile away, one of the oldest cemeteries in Killarney. It was a pleasant day and there was little wind and a warm sun. About 15 minutes later, I found myself in the courtyard of Muckross Abbey. Dominating everything around it was an enormous yew tree that must have been centuries old.

I started by inspecting the remains of what had once been a Franciscan monastery that was founded in the 15th century. Although the roof was completely gone, the walls appeared to be in a very good state of preservation. According to my guidebook, the monks of Muckross had been driven out in the 1650s by the forces of Oliver Cromwell.

Right next to the abbey is a graveyard which seemed to me to be in a very poor state of repair, but I could see from some of the newer stones that it was still being used as an active burial ground.

In the distance, I saw another gravedigger. Since I had several questions, I called out to him, but he either didn't hear me or didn't feel like talking because he ran away as I approached. I thought to myself what an impudent fellow, and then resumed my inspection of the tombstones.

Again, there were Celtic crosses everywhere – some were quite tall, and those I believed were called high crosses. The carvings on them were a marvel to behold, featuring bands of sinuous crisscrossing lines which I knew were a major characteristic of Gaelic art. Many of them were adorned with symbols. I recognized a few of them such as a ship that I suppose was intended to indicate the deceased had been a mariner. Unfortunately, there were whole hosts of icons – anchors, harps, lambs and many others, including an ankh, and an American dollar sign, which I thought odd and whose meaning eluded me altogether.

Once again, nothing struck me as being particularly unusual or out of place, and since it was nearing dinnertime, I decided to hike back to the hotel and enjoy a glass of claret and a cigar before deciding what to eat for supper.

I had just made my way back to the yew tree, when I saw the gravedigger that I had spotted earlier, sitting on a rock nearby and smoking a cigarette.

"I should like a word with you, my good fellow," I said.

"How many I be of assistance to such a fine gentleman as yourself?" he asked.

He sat there rather insolently, holding his shovel in one hand and his cigarette in the other. He appeared to be quite tall and with that flaming red hair that is a characteristic of so many of the Irish.

"Have there been any new burials here recently?"

"There's always someone going in the ground. People die, they come here, and me and my mates we bury 'em."

"Have you buried anyone in the last two weeks?"

"Why do you want to know?"

"I am asking on behalf of a friend of mine," I replied.

"Well, tell your friend to ask me himself," he said, and with that he ground out his cigarette and started to walk away.

"I am not done with you, my good man," I replied. "And there may be something in it for you, if you will help me."

"Let me see," he said rubbing his chin thoughtfully, we buried three women this week and a man and a woman last week. The stones aren't in place yet. Are you happy now, m'lord?" he asked holding out his hand.

"Indeed, I am," I said slipping him a few shillings.

"Well then, I'm glad I could be of service," he said with a bow and a rather obvious smirk.

As I walked back to the hotel, I wondered how Holmes was possibly going to locate the grave in which the stone had been hidden. Despite my best efforts in three different graveyards, I had seen nothing even remotely suggesting a clue.

After I had reached the hotel, I went up to my room, washed up and changed my clothes before heading downstairs to the dining room.

As I sat there perusing the menu, I was torn between several different entrees. I was leaning toward the stew when suddenly Holmes appeared at my table.

Sitting opposite me, he suggested, "I should try the stew if I were you. I think you'll find it a bit more satisfying, and certainly more filling, than either the fish or the lamb."

I was so glad to see my friend that I almost exclaimed "Holmes, how are you?"

Restraining myself, I simply said, "It's good to see you, and you are right. I will try the stew,"

"Excellent choice," he remarked, and then looking at me, he asked, "And did you learn anything on your visits to Killegy and Muckross Abbey?"

Chapter 36 – Killarney, Feb. 26

They rode in silence for the first half of the trip and then Kathleen suddenly broke the stillness, asking, "Denis, are you sure that you want to do this?"

"Not at all," he replied, "but I am tired of doing nothing. I think it imperative that we force the issue."

"You understand that we are not negotiating from a position of strength," she said. "We are hoping to leverage our possession of the stone into a promise from King Edward – something we haven't able to do thus far."

"What else are we to do?"

"Go back to Clonakilty and live our lives," she replied. "Trying to bluff them into surrendering our freedom isn't going to work. We stole the stone. We have it. Let's just be content with a small victory over the British. After all, if they try to crown their King with a counterfeit Coronation Stone, we can embarrass them in front of the world. And that might garner us more sympathy than any misguided attempt on your part to pretend that we are strong when we are not."

"So I'm misguided now?" Lyons asked. "That wasn't what you said when I first broached the plan."

"No, you're right," she said. "I thought it brilliant then and I still do, but I think you're letting your ego blind you to the reality of the situation."

Stung by her words, he could only say, "All I can ask is that you trust me, Kathleen. We have come this far – to quit now – I don't know if I could live with myself."

Grudgingly, she found herself saying, "I will support you, Dennis, but I want you to know that I think you are wrong."

"Oh *Mo Chuisle*, thank you," he said.

"I've asked you not to call me that," she said. "And if you do it again, you'll have to recognize Mr. Sherlock Holmes by yourself."

"My apologies, Kathleen. But you know how I feel."

"All too well," she replied, "and I wish I felt different, but I don't Denis. We are friends, comrades-in-arms, nothing more. I'm sorry."

"No apology is necessary, but if you should have a change of heart…," he left the sentence unfinished.

"You'll be waiting, I know," she said.

The exchange seemed to have cleared the air, and Lyons began to focus on the task at hand.

He was outlining things in his mind, when suddenly Kathleen asked, "And what will you do, if we should encounter Mr. Holmes?"

"I will endeavor to bring him over to our way of thinking."

"And if that should fail?"

"Then I will tell him, 'Mr. Holmes, we have the stone. If you will not side with us perhaps you can persuade the powers that be in England to consider our position. After all, it seems to me that you need the stone far more badly than we do. For you, it has meaning. For you, it embodies centuries of tradition. For us, it is nothing more than a bargaining chip. If we lose it, so be it."

"I like the sound of that," she said. "When you think logically and refuse to allow your emotions to override your common sense, you can be quite convincing."

Flattered by her praise, Lyons could only manage a quiet, "Thank you, Kathleen."

A few minutes later, the conductor announced that Killarney was the next stop.

"How long do you plan to stay here?" asked Kathleen.

"It's a rather larger city than Clonakilty. I should say that if we fail to encounter Holmes or Watson within three days, we can return home knowing that the stone is safe.

"If I cannot meet with Holmes and force the issue, then I will be guided by your counsel and settle for my symbolic victory."

While Kathleen secretly hoped that they would not encounter the detective, she was beginning to have serious misgivings about the entire expedition.

After the train pulled into Killarney, she and Lyons checked into their hotel. She was staying on the second floor and he on the third. Having gotten settled, they decided to have a late lunch before paying a visit to the cemetery.

As they exited the hotel after dining, Lyons said, "Muckross Abbey is about a mile away. We can either get a carriage or hope this good weather continues and walk."

"I've never been to Killarney. Let's walk," she said.

As they strolled through the streets, she stopped several times to look into various shop windows.

Although he was anxious to get to the graveyard, Lyons indulged her. "After all," he thought, "she has been a faithful companion and a good friend – and there is always the chance that she may change her mind."

After several visits to various shops, it was nearing twilight when they finally found themselves at the entrance to Muckross Abbey. The graveyard was deserted save for a solitary figure, smoking a cigarette near the giant yew tree.

Lyons hoped he would leave, but it soon became obvious that he was a worker there rather than a visitor. Once that realization had sunk in, Lyons gave him no further thought.

After strolling about the graveyard for 30 minutes and examining the various tombstones, Lyons went to the graves that he always visited, and from that vantage point he could see that all appeared well with the stone.

Now that he could relax, he said to Kathleen, "I don't know about you, but window-shopping makes me terribly hungry. Why don't we treat ourselves to a nice dinner and perhaps there's a show we can take in after."

"That sounds delightful, Denis. And if truth be told, window-shopping has a similar effect on me."

As they walked back toward town with the sun setting, Lyons noticed the man was still sitting under the yew tree, shovel by his side, smoking yet another cigarette.

Without anything more than two glances at the man, Lyons promptly changed his mind and decided that a worker who didn't appear to be working at all was probably someone worth keeping an eye on.

Chapter 37 Killarney, Feb. 26-27

"Holmes, I've just changed my clothes. There's no mud on my boots for you to observe, no cigarette ash on my trousers, so how could you possibly know where I've been all day?"

He laughed and said, "Watson, sometimes the answer to the question is standing in plain sight."

"What on earth do you mean?"

"While not following you, I too have visited both Killegy and Muckross Abbey myself, and, as luck would have it, I arrived at both after you had departed."

"Yes," I sputtered, "but that still doesn't explain how you knew I was there?"

"Did you speak to anyone, Watson?"

And then it hit me, "The gravediggers!" I exclaimed.

I watched as Holmes smiled at me, nodded and said, "Exactly. And by the way, you might have been a bit more generous with Edgar; he has proven quite helpful."

"Who on Earth is Edgar?"

"The fellow at Muckross Abbey. He thought you were rather high-handed."

"What?"

"I am not done with you, my good man," said Holmes, imitating my tone with the gravedigger perfectly.

In spite of myself, I had to laugh and Holmes joined me.

"And this Edgar fellow, is he in your employ?"

"As I said, thus far he has proven to be a tremendous help. His knowledge of local customs and traditions – especially regarding burials and tombstones has proven invaluable. I hope to find out in the very near future just how accurate his observations have been."

"What do you mean?"

"We were incredibly lucky today. It seems that shortly after you left Muckross Abbey but before I arrived, a young couple visited the cemetery. The woman was said to be quite attractive with long auburn hair. Her companion was tall and thin. Both appeared to be in their thirties. Sound like anyone you might know?"

"Kathleen Donnelly and Denis Lyons! Did they visit a particular grave?"

"Indeed, they did," replied Holmes.

"So then you know where the stone is!" I exclaimed.

"I'm afraid not, my friend, but I do have a much better idea. I should like to think that we are getting extremely close."

At that moment, the waiter arrived with our dinner. After he had left, Holmes said, "No more talk of that tonight. Tell me what you thought of the Herbert tomb at Killegy."

We spent the rest of the evening talking about what I had done and seen that day, and although I tried to steer the conversation back to the stone on more than one occasion, Holmes was having none of it.

The next morning, I knocked on Holmes' door for breakfast, but there was no answer.

After I had been seated in the dining room, I asked the waiter if he had seen my dinner companion from the evening before.

He replied that he had. He said that my friend had come down about an hour earlier, eaten a light breakfast and then departed.

When I had finished my own meal, I made my way to the front desk and asked if there were any messages for me. After checking, the clerk handed me an envelope. It was addressed to J.H.W. in a script that I knew to be Holmes'.

Upon opening the letter, I read.

"Watson,

I have high hopes of bringing this business to a conclusion tonight. May I suggest that you spend the day enjoying the sights of Killarney, but I must stress that you avoid both Killegy and Muckross Abbey and their environs at all costs. I have it on good authority that Ross Castle on the other side of Lough Leane is worth a visit, and since it is a locale that may yet come into play, a full report of the structure and its surroundings and defenses may prove invaluable. I have

reserved the hotel's small private dining room for this evening.
I shall meet you there at 7.

    S.H."

I must confess that I was more than a bit put out at not being included in Holmes' plans, but since I was well-acquainted with my friend's methods, my fit of pique soon passed.

With several hours to kill, I told the concierge that I was hoping to visit Ross Castle. He informed me that it was less than three miles away. As the warmer weather was still with us, I set out on foot for the castle, which I reached after a walk of about 45 minutes.

I will admit that initially I found myself terribly underwhelmed by the structure. However, after securing the services of an attractive young woman as a guide, my opinion began to change as I found myself admiring the array of defenses for such an innocuous looking edifice.

She informed me that Ross Castle, which had been built during the Middle Ages, featured a tower that had been surrounded by a square bawn, where the livestock had once grazed, and which, in turn, was defended by round corner towers on each end.

"The castle is constructed of stacked and mortared stone with thick walls and includes five inner stories plus the roof," she said.

At every level, one seemed to encounter another method for eliminating attackers. The front entrance was actually a small anteroom that could be secured by an iron grill or "yett." Pointing up, she said, the chief feature of this room was a "murder hole," allowing those defending the castle to attack anyone who managed to make it into the room from above.

The spiral staircase in the front left corner had been constructed in a clockwise direction. I knew that this had been done so that attackers ascending the stairs would, in most cases, have their swords in their right hands. Thus attacking and parrying would be impeded because of the wall while those defending, facing down, would have their swords swinging at the outer part of the staircase giving them a distinct advantage. Another little nicety, I gleaned from my guide, was that the stairs had been deliberately constructed of uneven heights to interfere with an attacker's stance and gait.

As we ascended, she told me that the castle also boasted two machiolations, which are stone structures at the top of the castle that jut out from the wall with a hole in the bottom. At Ross Castle, one can be found over the front door and another on the back wall. The one at the front would allow those under siege to drop stones or boiling oil on attackers at the front door, the only entrance to the castle.

Finally, we arrived at the roof. Pointing to the parapet at roof level, she told me that it was "crenellated" and featured a series of ups or "merlons" and downs or "crenels." Defenders could conceal themselves behind the merlons while counterattacking by firing arrows or guns through the crenels.

Looking east from the roof of the castle across Lough Leane, which glistened in the bright sunlight, I imagined that I could make out what I believed were the very top branches of the yew tree at Muckross Abbey. The thought gave me pause, and I wondered how Holmes might be faring.

After examining every inch of the castle, I looked at my watch and saw that it was just past three. I had no idea why or how this castle might figure into Holmes' investigation, but I had taken copious notes as my friend had requested, should he need them.

I decided that I had better start heading back to the hotel. Although dinner was at 7, I had worked up quite an appetite. I thought I might enjoy some sort of light repast before the evening meal.

I gave my guide a generous gratuity, which brought a smile to her face, and then I headed back in the direction of Killarney.

As I walked, I tried to imagine how the events of the evening might play out.

Although we were meeting our quarry in a public place, I found myself unable to escape a terrible sense of foreboding that had intruded into my thoughts, and like an unwelcome guest, refused to leave.

Chapter 38 – Killarney, Feb. 27

The next morning, Lyons told Kathleen he had some business to take care of, but that he would join her for lunch.

He took the train to Kenmare where he met with Santry.

"So far everything appears to be in order," Lyons said. "Kathleen and I visited the cemetery yesterday, and the only unusual thing I saw was a worker lounging about under the yew tree."

"What was odd about that?" asked Santry.

"We were there for about an hour. I saw him when we entered and again when we were leaving. At first, I was inclined to ignore him since I believe that he works there."

"You are sure it wasn't Holmes?" asked Santry.

"I am, unless Holmes can add several inches to his stature and has dyed his hair bright red, No, I do not think that it was he."

"He hoodwinked us all once," reminded Santry.

"Please don't remind me. If everyone knew, our *faux pas* would be on a par with the Cork Catastrophe."

Lyons continued, "At any rate, we will return to the cemetery this afternoon, and if I see him lounging about, I may well ask you to have a chat with him tomorrow."

"If that's what it takes," said Santry, flexing his muscles as he stretched.

"You've seen nothing unusual here?" asked Lyons.

"Nothing," replied Santry. "This village is so quiet, it makes Clonakilty look positively exhilarating."

"Only two more days," said Lyons. "If you don't hear from me by noon tomorrow, head home, and I will meet you in Clonakilty to plan our next move."

"Right," said Santry.

"I'm back to Killarney," said Lyons, who shook his old friend's hand and then headed for the train station.

During the short ride to Killarney, Lyons tried to anticipate the argument that he knew he would have with Kathleen, and then inspiration hit. He had finally devised a method that might bring the issue to a head.

After disembarking from the train, he headed to the hotel, where he had arranged to meet her for lunch.

As they ate, they discussed what their next steps might be, and once again, they ended up agreeing to disagree.

Lyons was still intent on forcing the issue while Kathleen remained content to settle for a symbolic victory.

"Suppose I developed had a new plan. Would you hear me out?"

"Of course," she replied.

"It's a bit hazardous, but, you know what they say, 'No risk, no reward.'"

"So what's the idea?" she asked impatiently.

"Thus far, very few people know that we have the stone. What if we can make getting the stone back a *cause celebre* for the English people?"

"How do you propose to do that?"

"We dig up the stone and carry it to an obvious Irish landmark, such as Kilmainham Gaol in Dublin. Then we arrange to have photographs taken and send them to every important newspaper – both here in Europe and America. We tell them that just as the Irish are being held captive by the British, we are holding the Stone of Destiny prisoner. When we are free, we will liberate the stone and return it to its 'rightful' home. If the British really want their stone back, they will have to give us our freedom."

"Denis, that is inspired!" she exclaimed.

"Do you think it will work?" he asked.

"I do," she replied. "I especially like the idea of involving the Americans. I should think they will understand our plight better than anyone else, and there are many powerful Irishmen in America who may be able to bring some pressure to bear on His Majesty's government."

"We will have to be very careful retrieving the stone and transporting it," he said.

"That's where the Brotherhood comes in," she said. "We will use the coffin to transport it to Dublin, and we'll let those along the way know we are coming. We'll have a squadron of men on the train, and if anyone should try to take it from us, they'll get what for," she said.

"It's going to take some planning," he said, "but I should think we can be ready within a week."

Her smile was all he needed by way of encouragement.

"Yesterday, we window-shopped," he said. "Today, I think we should buy you something pretty – as a sort of celebration."

Feeling exhilarated, they set out for Clovers Lane and the shopping district. As they walked, they chatted and then they stopped in front of a small jewelry store.

"I know you would never let me give you a Claddagh ring," said Lyons, "but I was wondering – given everything you've done – if I might be permitted to buy you a silver 'warrior' Celtic cross pendant. I saw one in here on one of my trips that looks a great deal like the stone we are using."

"That would be lovely," she said.

After they had made their purchase, they set out for the cemetery. As they passed the yew tree, Lyons was relieved to see that there was no one lounging about.

In fact, they appeared to be the only ones in the entire cemetery. "That's odd," he thought, "You would think on such a lovely afternoon, there would be others here." But there was no one to be seen.

As they made their way to the graves that Lyons always visited, the ones from which he had an unobstructed view of the stone's hiding place, he could sense that something was different. It was almost imperceptible, but something had definitely changed in the graveyard. Still, he would have been hard-pressed to say exactly what it was.

As he stood at his parents' grave, something fluttering in the distance caught his eye. Looking about and seeing no one, he edged a few feet closer to the Celtic cross above the Stone of Destiny.

With his improved point of view, he could see that there was something hanging from the cross. It was white and occasionally a breeze would lift it from the stone.

Moving ever closer, he came to realize that it was an envelope that had been secured to the cross by a piece of string.

Now that he was only 20 feet or so from the stone, he could also see that the sod in front of the cross had been greatly disturbed. It was obvious that someone had been digging.

Sprinting to the cross, he grasped the envelope and turning it over, he was stunned to discover that it was addressed to him.

At that point, Kathleen caught up to him and said, "What is that?"

"It appears to be a letter addressed to me. I am afraid we are undone."

"Open it," she said, "See what it says."

Peeling back the flap, Lyons extracted a single piece of paper that had been folded in half. After unfolding it, he read aloud:

"Dear Mr. Lyons,

I hope that you and Miss Donnelly will be able to join Dr. Watson and me for dinner tonight at 7. I have reserved the small private dining room in the Railway Hotel. We have much to discuss.

Sincerely yours,

Sherlock Holmes"

Chapter 39 – Killarney, Feb. 27

When I met Holmes at about a quarter to seven, I was immediately struck by the fact that he seemed in a peculiar mood.

It was difficult to tell whether he was more apprehensive or jubilant.

He would glance at his watch frequently, and as the appointed hour neared, he said more to himself than to me, "I have baited the trap – and quite carefully. Could I have made a misstep?"

Throwing himself into a chair, he sat there in silence. As he steepled his hands in front of him, I could see him reviewing each step of his plan in his mind.

A few minutes later, I heard a familiar woman's voice say, "We are looking for the private dining room. I believe we are expected."

Turning to my friend, I saw him rise to his feet, struggling to conceal a smile.

Less than a minute later, Kathleen Donnelly and Denis Lyons were ushered into the room.

"Ah, Miss Donnelly, it is so nice to see you again! I believe you remember my friend, Dr. Watson?"

"Indeed, I do," she said smiling at me.

She continued, "It is nice to see you again, Doctor. I could only wish the circumstances were different."

"And Mr. Lyons, you are looking well," said Holmes.

"Well you look quite different from the last time, I saw you, Paul," replied Lyons, with more than a hint of sarcasm in his voice.

"Yes, I suppose I do," said Holmes.

"At least this time around, I can shake your hand," said my friend, extending his hand toward Lyons.

Ignoring it, Lyons said, "Have you invited us here to gloat?"

"What did my letter say?" asked Holmes.

"You know damn well what it said," replied Lyons.

"Humor me please, and read it aloud," said Holmes.

Pulling it from his pocket, Lyons read:

"Dear Mr. Lyons,

I hope that you and Miss Donnelly will be able to join Dr. Watson and me for dinner tonight at 7. I have reserved the small private dining room in the Railway Hotel. We have much to discuss.

Sincerely yours,

Sherlock Holmes"

"And so we do," said my friend genially. "I feel compelled to warn you before we proceed, your futures may well depend upon your actions and your answers here tonight. Now, let us eat, shall we?"

As we sat at the table, there was an incredibly awkward silence. Finally, Lyons looked at Holmes and said, "I can only assume from the way the grave was dug up that you have recovered the Stone of Destiny."

"Yes," said Holmes imperturbably. "It is on its way back to Westminster Abbey as we speak."

At that point, the soup arrived, and Holmes informed us, "I have taken the liberty of ordering for everyone. If you should object to anything, including the mulligatawny soup, please feel free to order something else. I certainly will not take it amiss, and neither will the kitchen, I can assure you."

"What is this? A condemned man's last meal?" asked Lyons.

"Not at all," replied Holmes. "It is a chance for you to tell me why you did what you did."

Over the next hour, Lyons made the case for Irish freedom. He was an eloquent spokesman, and his words were imbued with the passion of a true believer.

Finally he concluded, "So I devised this scheme because we needed to get the monarchy to listen to us, to really hear us."

"Just how far were you prepared to go?" asked Holmes.

"Honestly, I don't know," replied Lyons. "I will admit that violence against you crossed my mind."

"I'm afraid it did more than cross your mind," my friend said. "I haven't forgotten those two toughs waiting for me outside my lodgings."

"They were told only to scare you," said Lyons, "Still, I think you had the better of both of them that day."

"Yes, I suppose I did."

"Would you have killed me?" my friend asked suddenly.

Without hesitating Lyons replied, "Again, I must admit that the thought crossed my mind on more than one occasion, but I will tell you quite honestly that I do not know."

"Mr. Holmes," said Miss Donnelly, who had been silent for a long time. "Denis is a good man. He is loyal to his friends and his cause, but there are lines that I do not believe he would cross, and murder is certainly one of them."

"Thank you, Miss Donnelly," said Holmes chivalrously. "Again, your honesty impresses me."

As the waiter poured coffee, Holmes asked, "Do you mind if I smoke?"

"Not at all," replied Lyons.

After a prolonged silence, during which Holmes lit a second cigarette, Lyons finally said, "Mr. Holmes, I am ready to accept whatever punishment you may have in store for me, but can you find it in your heart to spare Kathleen? She has the soul of a warrior, and prison would kill her."

"Prison," laughed Holmes. "Who said anything about prison?"

"Then what is to become of us?" asked Lyons.

"That sir is entirely up to you and Miss Donnelly."

"You're not arresting us?"

"Mr. Lyons, I was employed to recover the Coronation Stone. Nothing in my instructions included apprehending those who made off with it. I am not a policeman. I do not arrest people. However, I feel compelled to tell you that earlier in the evening, I believe I did see two inspectors from Scotland Yard sitting at a table by the window in the main dining room."

"We are free to go?" asked Lyons incredulously.

"You are," replied Holmes.

"I do not know what to say."

"I do," interjected Miss Donnelly. "Thank you, Mr. Holmes – and Dr. Watson. Thank you both very much."

"May I offer one bit of advice?" asked Holmes.

"Of course," said Miss Donnelly.

"I have scant interest in politics. However, after listening to Mr. Lyons, I am certain that there is merit to your cause. Continue the good fight. Everyone deserves to be free. So I encourage you to stick to your principles, but you must oblige me in one small area."

"Anything, Mr. Holmes," said Lyons.

"I beg of you, please try to refrain from stealing any more English relics."

At that we all laughed, and then we shook hands all around, and Lyons and Miss Donnelly departed.

"Well that was quite magnanimous of you, Holmes."

"Not at all, Watson. I think it was fairly pragmatic."

"In what respect?"

"If you take two attractive young people and imprison them for fighting for their freedom, you've not only created two martyrs, but you have put a face on the cause of Irish liberty – and a very attractive face, I might add. Better, they should return home and continue their struggle from the obscurity of Clonakilty."

"They do make a handsome couple," I observed.

Holmes looked at me and then laughed heartily, "She is not for him. I can assure you of that, Watson."

Before I could press the issue, he continued, "I do not know how the strained relations between England and Ireland may be improved or even if they can be. That's a job better suited for Mycroft."

"Now, old friend, let us get a good night's sleep. We have a great many things to do in the morning."

"Such as?" I asked.

"Well, the first thing we have to do is get a crew of men together and then go and dig up the Coronation Stone."

Chapter 40 – Clonakilty, Feb. 27-28

The train ride from Killarney to Clonakilty was spent largely in silence.

Finally, at one point, Lyons asked, "Where did we go wrong? How could he have located the only grave in a country filled with churchyards?"

"I am sure I do not know, but at least we now understand why the Crown hired him to recover the stone. He may be the only one who could have solved the puzzle that you presented him."

"Yes. I suppose you're right. Reluctantly, we must tip our hat to Mr. Sherlock Holmes, and should we decide to essay a similar undertaking, we must pray that he remains on the sidelines rather than entering the fray."

* * *

The next morning, I awoke at eight and after dressing. I lightly knocked on Holmes' door. When there was no answer, I descended and found him sitting in the dining room, perusing the morning paper.

"There you are," he greeted me. "Another 10 minutes, and I was coming up to wake you."

"What time did you get up?"

"I arose at 6, dressed and then set about sending a series of telegrams."

"Before we go any further, I want to know how you discovered where the Coronation Stone was being concealed."

"Well, as I told you earlier, I wasn't exactly certain where it was hidden until Mr. Lyons told me."

"He told you!" I exclaimed. "When?"

"Do you remember when I asked Mr. Lyons to read my letter?"

"Of course."

"When he was reading, he told me exactly where he had concealed the stone."

"I heard him say nothing of the kind!"

"I'm sorry, old man. I am pulling your leg a bit. Let me backtrack a bit."

"I had narrowed the possible hiding place to either Killegy Cemetery or Muckross Abbey. I was inclined to think it was the latter, but Lyons is so clever that I couldn't totally discount the former either.

"After thoroughly examining the tombstones in both, I had reduced the possibilities to five – three in Killegy and two at Muckross. Had Mr. Lyons surveyed the entire cemetery – and it is a good thing he did not – he would have come across a similar note hanging from another tombstone.

"I say similar because the wording in each was almost identical. But each missive was just slightly different from the others. Do you remember the last sentence of the letter Lyons read?"

Thinking back, I said, "I believe it was 'We have much to discuss'."

"That's it exactly," said Holmes. "That it was not a P.S. or that I didn't use the phrase 'a great deal' told me it was the grave marker to which we will we make our way shortly."

After breakfast, we took a carriage to Muckross Abbey where we found six men and a wagon waiting for us at the gate, along with the gravedigger, Edgar, whom Holmes had befriended.

The men were dressed as workers, but one stepped forward. "Mr. Holmes?" he inquired.

"I am Sherlock Holmes, and this is my good friend, Dr. John Watson."

Saluting, he said, "I am Captain Wayne Miller of His Majesty's Royal Navy, and these men are all officers from my crew."

"A bit inland aren't you captain?" I asked.

"The only response I can make to that, doctor, is that we were sent here because our ship was anchored in Cobh, and we are not known to the locals. I was told there was the possibility of an 'incident,' which is why we are dressed as laborers, and not in our uniforms."

"Very good, captain," said Holmes. "Now if you will follow me."

Turning to Edgar, Holmes asked, "No one has been here this morning?"

"No sir," he replied.

"And the shovels?"

"They are in the wagon," said Edgar.

"You have done well, my friend," said Holmes, pressing some notes into the man's hand.

"Now, gentlemen. It's this way."

Holmes led us to a remote corner of the cemetery and pointing to a grave, marked by a Celtic cross, said, "I believe that is the one we want."

The men set about digging, and I said to Holmes, "I pray that you are right."

A few minutes later, I heard the sound of a shovel striking wood.

"Easy now," said Holmes, "We don't want to damage it."

After another 15 minutes, the men were able to slide ropes under the coffin.

As they started to lift, one of them said, "By God, this is heavy. What's in here?"

When they had extricated it from the grave and lowered it to the ground, Holmes took a crowbar from the wagon and began to ease the lid off.

After he had lifted the top a few inches, he peered inside, looked at me and smiled.

After re-securing the lid, he turned to the captain and said. "Take this to railway station. We will meet you there shortly. I just have two more bits of business to which I must attend."

"As you wish Mr. Holmes," said Captain Miller.

Looking at me, Holmes said, "On second thought, Watson, why don't you accompany them? I'll retrieve your belongings from the hotel and meet you forthwith. Having come this far, I am loath to let it out of my sight, so you must be my eyes."

And so it was that I accompanied Captain Miller and his crew to the Killarney station where we were joined by Holmes about 25 minutes later.

"I settled our bill, and then I had to wire Mycroft," he said.

About 30 minutes later, we boarded the Cork, Brandon and South Coast Railway, and just over three hours after that we disembarked in Cork, made our way to Cobh and boarded the HMS Diadem.

The next day we were back in Britain, landing at London.

An armed contingent of 10 men met us after we disembarked, and the leader told Holmes that a private carriage was waiting to take us and our cargo to Westminster Abbey.

We watched as the men loaded the coffin on a wagon and then escorted it to the abbey.

When we arrived at the church, we drove up the same path to the side entrance that we had taken a few weeks earlier.

George Bradley was waiting for us at the door.
"It is so good to see you, Mr. Holmes," he said. "Mr. Dodge and I brought the Coronation Chair back into the chapel this morning after closing the church, and I have a carpenter waiting inside."

"Splendid," said my friend.

The men then lowered the coffin to the ground and opened it.

For the first time, I saw the Coronation Stone in its entirety.

Using the embedded rings, the men then lifted it on two pipes and carried it inside the church.

Holmes followed them as far as the door. He paused there to examine something and when he returned, he said, "They have installed new locks that might even give me pause,

Watson. Also, they have hired a night watchman. I think we can go home now."

As we rode to Baker Street, Holmes penned a quick note.

"This is to Mycroft. I told him we would meet him at the Diogenes Club tomorrow evening. I don't know about you, old man, but I am exhausted and anxious to sleep in my own bed."

That was a sentiment that I heartily shared.

Chapter 41 – London, March 1

The next evening Holmes and I took a cab to the Diogenes Club. After a few moments, we were joined in the Stranger's Room by Mycroft.

"Well done," he said to us as he entered. "Both His Majesty and the Home Office have asked me to extend their congratulations as well."

After settling himself into a chair, he looked at Holmes and said, "Now, please tell me how you managed to locate the one grave in an entire country that had served as the hiding place for the Coronation Stone."

"I've been rather curious about that myself," I added.

Smiling, Holmes began to relate the tale, occasionally omitting a fact here or there and at times filling in parts that were unknown to me.

"What puzzles me," I interrupted at one point, "is how you managed to narrow it down to just those two cemeteries."

"I must confess, I owe that bit of intelligence to Mycroft, at least indirectly. We knew that Lyons had resided in Killarney before he moved to Clonakilty. I was inclined to think that he might conceal the stone in a cemetery in that area. I wired Mycroft and asked him to find out where Lyons' parents had been buried.

"When I received the wire that said his parents' graves were in Muckross Abbey, that became the focal point of my investigation. However, I couldn't dismiss Killegy entirely, both because Lyons was certainly crafty enough to conceal it in a nearby graveyard and because Mycroft also informed me that his maternal grandparents had been buried there.

"In the end, however, he decided to conceal it within sight of his parents' grave, so while it was hidden, it was also in plain sight," said Holmes, casting a sideways glance at me.

Continuing, he said, "I thought it would be fairly close by, and I surmised that it would be in front of and possibly off to the side of his parents' grave, rather than behind it. Now that I was able to confine my search to specific areas of the graveyards at Killegy and Muckross, it only remained for me to find the gravestone that didn't belong.

"Watson, you remember that at one point I had inquired about tombstones being stolen and learned that several had gone missing in the north of Ireland."

I nodded.

Holmes continued, "At the time, I simply dismissed it, thinking the thefts were the result of religious tensions. However, the more I thought about it, the more I considered that a tombstone would serve as the perfect bit of camouflage.

"Since I was fairly certain they had used a grave

marker so as to help the site blend it, I began to consult with several local artisans about the symbols that appear on tombstones and the style in which they are carved. I knew that looking at the stones was going to be an exercise in futility unless I knew exactly what I was looking for."

"I can attest to that," I said,

Holmes smiled at me and then continued, "As you know, carving techniques, like so many other things, differ greatly from region to region. If they had truly hidden it with a tombstone brought from the north, I expected to find some differences on the tombstone that guarded the grave.

"After a thorough examination of both cemeteries, paying particular attention to the markers near Lyons' parents' and grandparents' graves, I returned to the local monument maker. I had noticed one rather distinctive symbol that appeared on just a few stones and I was hoping that any significant difference might allow me to prove my hypothesis."

"And what symbol is that?" Mycroft asked.

Turning to me, Holmes said, "Watson, I am certain that during your recent graveyard sojourns you came across the inscription 'IHS' on any number of markers."

"Indeed, I did," I replied. "I saw a great many of those symbols, and I was wondering what it might mean."

Holmes said, "Popular since medieval times 'IHS' can be translated in several ways, including variously as *Iesous* a rendering of the Greek orthography for 'Jesus' or as *Iesus*

Hominum Salvator, Jesus, saviour of mankind or even as '*In Hoc Signo [Vince]'* (In this sign, you shall conquer).

"I am assured by the artisans with whom I have spoken that it is easily one of the most common ideograms to be found in Irish cemeteries. More important, however, is the fact that it can be carved in several different manners, and, as you might expect, the popularity of each style has ebbed and flowed with the passage of time. Moreover, they also differ from one section of Ireland to another.

"Do you recall the ideogram on the stone, Watson?"

"Yes, I do. I must admit that it struck me as rather odd because I had never seen anything exactly like it before."

"My point exactly," said Holmes. "Lyons obtained a stone from the proper period – the mid-19th century – and placed it among other stones from that period. Perhaps he knew the workmanship was slightly different, but then you must remember that he never expected to get caught."

"They never do," I laughed.

"At any rate, the stone Lyons had chosen is emblazoned with what the stone masons call an 'entwined IHS.' and both artisans with whom I spoke said the first time they had ever seen a carving like that was around 1870 on various visits to the north, specifically Belfast, which is only about 40 miles from Armagh.

"It's a fairly distinctive symbol that could easily be

mistaken for the American dollar sign. Fortunately, while the symbol appears to have been quite popular in the north for some years, it is only recently that it has it made its way south.

"I returned to Killegy where I found three instances of the 'entwined IHS' and Muckross where I found just two others. I discovered that on all of the surrounding stones where the IHS did appear, it was either a 'plain IHS' or an IHS with a crucifix.

"When I have time, I may compose a monograph on the subject," said my friend.

"Bravo," said Mycroft. "Now, where are Mr. Lyons and his associates?"

"I would think they are in Clonakilty," said Holmes.

"And was he suitably grateful that he was not to be taken into custody?"

"Indeed," said Holmes. "I rather think this escapade will soon fade in their memories. After all, no one likes to sit around and reminisce about a failure."

"I agree," said Mycroft. "And you said you have something for me?"

"Yes," said Holmes, handing his brother a folded sheet of foolscap.

After examining it, Mycroft said, "All things considered, this is quite reasonable. I shall have checks deposited in your accounts tomorrow."

"Thank you," said my friend.

After chatting for a few minutes more, Mycroft said, "I hope you will excuse me, but I do some have business to which I must attend."

On the way home in the cab, I said to Holmes, "Is he putting a check in my account as well."

"Indeed," said Holmes. "After everything you have endured and sacrificed, I thought you deserved some small degree of recompense."

"Thank you," I said. "That really wasn't necessary though."

"I think it is actually intended to buy your silence, Watson. Mycroft has made it quite clear that this particular adventure is not to end up in The Strand."

"You have my word," I said. "However, it will certainly makes its way into my tin dispatch box in case I should need to refer to it at some point in the future."

"As long as it remains there," said Holmes.

Epilogue

Although Holmes had recovered the Coronation Stone in fairly short order, it would be more than a year later before the coronation of Edward VII and his wife, Alexandra, would take place in Westminster Abbey.

Originally scheduled for June 26, 1902 – no explanation was ever given for the lengthy delay – the ceremony had to be postponed on very short notice when the King was taken ill with an abdominal abscess that required immediate surgery.

There was some speculation that since Victoria's own coronation had been a rather modest affair that had been eclipsed by the successes of both her Golden and Diamond Jubilees, that there was a certain expectation King Edward's coronation would be an expression of the nation's status as a great imperial power.

Finally, in December of 1901 an Executive Coronation Committee was formed. The group was led by Viscount Esher, who reportedly worked quite closely with the King in arranging the agenda for the event.

To his credit, it was Esher who had organized Queen Victoria's Diamond Jubilee in 1897. Given the success of that event and the fact that Esher was an instrumental figure in pushing for the renewed enthusiasm for royal ceremonial, he seemed the obvious choice.

As the coronation day neared, Edward was described by reporters as "worn and pale" and relying a great deal on his cane.

On June 24, two days before the scheduled coronation, a telegram marked "OFFICIAL" was dispatched around the Empire. It contained the news that the coronation had to be postponed and that King Edward was to undergo an operation. Sometime later, a bulletin was released from the monarch's medical team, which informed the public:

"The King is suffering from perityphlitis. King Edward's condition on Saturday was so satisfactory that it was hoped that with care His Majesty would be able to go through the coronation ceremonies. On Monday evening a recrudescence became manifest, rendering a surgical operation necessary today."

It was undersigned by, among others, Lord Joseph Lister and Sir Frederick Treves.

In fact, it was later revealed that King Edward had been diagnosed with appendicitis, which at that time had an extremely high mortality rate.

Although operations for the condition were uncommon, surgery using the recently developed techniques of anaesthesia and antisepsis was possible.

The procedure was performed in the Music Room at Buckingham Palace, where Treves, supported by Lister, successfully treated the illness using the then-unconventional method of draining the abscess through an incision, and the monarch's health began to improve dramatically.

With the King's life saved, the coronation was moved to August 9, and Edward assumed the throne as so many of his predecessors had – sitting in the Coronation Chair above the Stone of Destiny in Westminster Abbey.

Author's note

The history of the Stone of Destiny as told in this book is as true as the history of any object whose origins are shrouded in mystery can be.

The important aspects are these: After it was taken to England by King Edward I in 1296 and installed in the Coronation Chair, every British monarch has sat in that chair and upon that stone when he or she has been invested.

Although the stone was to have been returned to Scotland in 1328 under the terms of the Treaty of Northhampton, riotous crowds prevented it from being removed from Westminster Abbey. So the Coronation Stone remained in England for another six centuries. Oddly enough, even when James VI of Scotland assumed the throne as James I of England, the stone remained in Westminster where Stuart kings and queens of Scotland sat upon it but at their coronations as kings and queens of England.

The only time the stone left England was in 1950 when a small group of Scottish students broke into Westminster on Christmas Eve and spirited the Stone of Scone back to Scotland. Unfortunately, the stone was broken into two pieces during their escapade, but it was repaired and four months later it was discovered by British police on the altar of Arbroath Abbey on April 11, 1951.

Finally, in 1996, as a symbolic gesture to growing dissatisfaction among Scots at the prevailing constitutional settlement, the British Conservative Government decided that the stone should be kept in Scotland when not in use at coronations. And so it was that on July 3, 1996, it was announced in the House of Commons that the stone would be returned to Scotland, and on Nov. 15, 1996, there was a ceremony at the border between representatives of the Home Office and the Scottish Office, after which it was transported to Edinburgh Castle.

The stone currently remains alongside the crown jewels of Scotland in the Crown Room. However, it will be returned to England on the occasion of a new monarch assuming the throne.

Finally, although the stone has far more ties to Scotland than Ireland, I felt that given the political climate of 1901, if anyone were going to steal the stone, it would be a group of Irish separatists, rather than Scottish nationalists.

Acknowledgements

I have said in the past that writing is a lonely task made easier by the encouragement and patience of the following who have supported and encouraged me in my endeavors.

I should be terribly remiss if I failed to thank my publisher, Steve Emecz, who makes the process painless, and Brian Belanger, whose skill as a cover designer is unmatched.

No book is complete without a solid line edit, and Deborah Annakin Peters provided that as well as a number of invaluable suggestions that improved the book immeasurably.

I also owe a debt to Bob Katz, a good friend and the finest Sherlockian I know, who prodded me on and suggested that if I were going to continue penning pastiches, I should try to remain true to the Canon in all respects, including length.

To Francine and Richard Kitts and Carol and Ron Fish, fine Sherlockians all, for their unflagging support and fellowship.

To my brother, Edward, and my sister, Arlene, who quite often had more faith in me than I had in myself.

Finally, to all those, and there are far too many to name, whose support for "The Vatican Cameos," made me see just what a great life I have and what incredible friends I am surrounded by.

To say that I am in their debt doesn't even begin to scratch the surface of my gratitude.

About the author

Richard T. Ryan is a native New Yorker, having been born and raised on Staten Island. He majored in English at St. Peter's College and pursued his graduate studies, concentrating on medieval literature, at the University of Notre Dame.

After teaching high school and college for several years, he joined the staff of the Staten Island Advance. He currently serves as the publications manager for that paper although he still prefers the title, news editor.

In addition to his first novel, "The Vatican Cameos: A Sherlock Holmes Adventure," he has written three trivia books, including "The Official Sherlock Holmes Trivia Book." He is also the author of "Deadly Relations," a mystery that was well-received during its two off-Broadway runs.

He is the very proud father of two children, Dr. Kaitlin Ryan Smith and Michael Ryan.

He has been married for 38 years to his wife, Grace, and continues to marvel at her incredible patience in putting up with him and his computer illiteracy.

He is currently at work on a Holmes short story and is planning his next novel.

Also from Richard T. Ryan

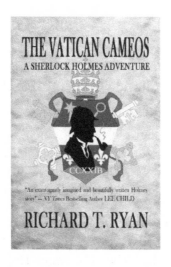

When the papal apartments are burgled in 1901, Sherlock Holmes is summoned to Rome by Pope Leo XIII. After learning from the pope that several priceless cameos that could prove compromising to the church, and perhaps determine the future of the newly unified Italy, have been stolen, Holmes is asked to recover them. In a parallel story, Michelangelo, the toast of Rome in 1501 after the unveiling of his Pieta, is tasked by Pope Alexander VI, the last of the Borgia pontiffs, with creating the cameos that will bedevil Holmes and the papacy four centuries later. For fans of Conan Doyle's immortal detective, the game is always afoot. However, the great detective has never encountered an adversary quite like the one with whom he crosses swords in "The Vatican Cameos."

"An extravagantly imagined and beautifully written Holmes story"
(Lee Child, NY Times Bestselling author, Jack Reacher series)

www.mxpublishing.com

Also from MX Publishing

MX Publishing is the world's largest specialist Sherlock Holmes publisher, with over a hundred titles and fifty authors creating the latest in Sherlock Holmes fiction and non-fiction.

From traditional short stories and novels to travel guides and quiz books, MX Publishing cater for all Holmes fans.

The collection includes leading titles such as *Benedict Cumberbatch In Transition* and *The Norwood Author* which won the 2011 Howlett Award (Sherlock Holmes Book of the Year).

MX Publishing also has one of the largest communities of Holmes fans on Facebook with regular contributions from dozens of authors.

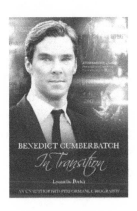

www.mxpublishing.com

Also from MX Publishing

"Phil Growick's, 'The Secret Journal of Dr Watson', is an adventure which takes place in the latter part of Holmes and Watson's lives. They are entrusted by HM Government (although not officially) and the King no less to undertake a rescue mission to save the Romanovs, Russia's Royal family from a grisly end at the hand of the Bolsheviks. There is a wealth of detail in the story but not so much as would detract us from the enjoyment of the story. Espionage, counterespionage, the ace of spies himself, double-agents, doublecrossers...all these flit across the pages in a realistic and exciting way. All the characters are extremely well-drawn and Mr. Growick, most importantly, does not falter with a very good ear for Holmesian dialogue indeed. Highly recommended. A five-star effort."
The Baker Street Society

www.mxpublishing.com

Also from MX Publishing

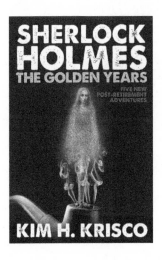

Sherlock Holmes lamented, "I fear that retirement will elude me." It surely does in this five story chronicle. The saga begins with The Bonnie Bag of Bones that lead the infamous duo on a not-so-merry chase into the mythical mountains of Scotland and ultimately to the "the woman" who is tangled within a mystery that has haunted Holmes for a quarter century. Curse of the Black Feather continues the adventure in which Holmes teams up with the Irregulars and a gypsy matriarch, to expose a diabolical "baby-farming" enterprise. Their quest arouses a vicious adversary, Ciarán Malastier, who has Holmes struggling for his very life. Maestro of Mysteries begins with a summons to Mycroft's office and ends with a deadly chase in Undertown, far beneath the streets of London. Malastier escapes, but only into the next adventure.

CPSIA information can be obtained
at www.ICGtesting.com
Printed in the USA
BVHW030713300720
584498BV00026B/28/J

9 781787 050822